"Schulman's startling brilliance and wry humor is everything."
—JACQUELINE WOODSON, author of *Another Brooklyn*

"*Maggie Terry* is the most beautiful, most bitter, most sweet, and all around best detective novel I've read in years. Precise, insightful, heartbreaking, and page turning—read this book, now."
—SARA GRAN, author of ***Claire DeWitt and the Bohemian Highway***

"*Maggie Terry* is day-after noir: the party is over, the neon burned out, and there's nothing to drink but cold-pressed kale juice. Clear-eyed and beautifully written, this novel is classic Schulman. She flenses and dissects the human condition, weighs every organ—how we connect, what forms the beating heart of a community—then magically breathes life back into the husk and helps it rise, reborn. *Maggie Terry* is a light shining in the waste, offering hope: where there are people, there is the possibility of connection, and together we can make it."
—NICOLA GRIFFITH, author of *So Lucky*

"*Maggie Terry* is inventive, boundary pushing, and absolutely electric. It centers women and queerness in the most exciting way, within a story you'll never want to stop reading. Sarah is a brilliant writer who navigates fiction with all the same nuance, depth, and authenticity we've come to expect from her groundbreaking nonfiction work. Get lost in this deeply engrossing novel."
—JILL SOLOWAY, creator of *Transparent*

"Entirely original and mixing many genres, this book is about imagining a way forward when there seems to be no way at all."
—KAITLYN GREENIDGE, author of ***We Love You, Charlie Freeman***

"A reverberating story of our times. Sarah Schulman is at the top of her very considerable powers in this deeply humane novel. It is profoundly, just stunningly good."
—KATHERINE V. FORREST, author of *High Desert*

"A psychological portrait of a woman trying to make her way back from the edge, and an inspiring one at that."
—DANNY CAINE, The Raven Book Store

ALSO BY SARAH SCHULMAN

Maggie

Terry

A NOVEL

SARAH SCHULMAN

FEMINIST PRESS
AT THE CITY UNIVERSITY OF NEW YORK
NEW YORK CITY

Published in 2018 by the Feminist Press
at the City University of New York
The Graduate Center
365 Fifth Avenue, Suite 5406
New York, NY 10016

feministpress.org

First Feminist Press edition 2018

This book was made possible thanks to a grant from New York State Council
on the Arts with the support of Governor Andrew M. Cuomo and the New York
State Legislature.

First printing September 2018

Cover and text design by Drew Stevens

Library of Congress Cataloging-in-Publication Data
Names: Schulman, Sarah, 1958- author.
Title: Maggie Terry / Sarah Schulman.
Description: New York, NY : Feminist Press, [2018]
Identifiers: LCCN 2018011665| ISBN 9781936932399 (softcover) | ISBN
    9781936932405 (ebook)
Subjects: LCSH: Political fiction. | GSAFD: Mystery fiction.
Classification: LCC PS3569.C5393 M34 2018 | DDC 813/.54--dc23
LC record available at https://lccn.loc.gov/2018011665

In memory of Thelma Wood

Maggie Terry

DAY ONE

WEDNESDAY, JULY 5, 2017

CHAPTER ONE

8:00 AM

Everyone was in a state of confusion because the president was insane. No one knew if a strategy drove the chaos, or if he was simply mad. The wide range of elected officials in charge of protecting the people was inadequate to the task. The system had created their status and yet that system no longer existed. But they were too complicit to go rogue. Seven months into the madness he gave his July 4 speech on a sweltering July 1, just to create more anxiety. Reading off of the teleprompter, he proclaimed that his nation would now say "Merry Christmas" instead of "Happy Holidays." He decreed that "Americans don't worship the government, we worship God." And he threatened war in the few spots on earth where one was not yet raging while trying to close down Amtrak. Muslim humans from six countries were banned for no reason that correlated to anything in reality. He proposed repeating universal health care without substituting something in its place. If he had ever paid taxes, he didn't want to pay any more. While rarely coherent, this man often repeated that he was "winning" and reminded his audience that he had already "won" and would continue to "win."

Social deterioration unfolded at breakneck speed. Only thirteen ambassadors had been appointed to take care of our relationships with the entire world; most of the governmental offices were empty. Public land was being divided and sold to the highest bidder. The poor, shaken planet earth was, herself, in revolt. Fires ravaged the world. So many people had been driven from their homes that the word *home* had been redefined as a memory, a myth of permanence.

Meanwhile, back in New York City, the subways either derailed with regularity or did not run at all. Landlines that had functioned during 9/11 and Hurricane Sandy were finally down because the cables had been chewed through by rats. A doctor walked into a hospital in the Bronx with an automatic weapon, murdered another doctor, and wounded six patients. Fireworks seemed redundant as everyone's bike was stolen.

As for Maggie Terry? To say she was *frightened* would be untrue, because the degradation of her specifically *personal* cliché betrayed a banality that was incompatible with either national calamity or simple fear. It was not *fear* per se, but the first experience of real trepidatious, hesitant terror coming embarrassingly late at the age of forty-two. Her timing could not have been worse, as her private disintegration mirrored that of her society. And this made her seem even more pathetic and small.

The reason it had previously taken four decades of blithe self-confidence until Maggie suddenly shattered was, of course, intoxication, and there is nothing more mundane. Addiction, like the sunrise, is known, predictable, useless, dependable, and a fact.

And yet, there are still revelations.

That first morning, Maggie's new place was not yet painted. There were no blinds on the windows. Boxes sat in a corner; there was no furniture. The refrigerator's medicinal hum was the room's only sign of function. Could she learn from her refrigerator and achieve its goal of preservation? The summer was hot as hell when hell lives in a studio apartment. Maggie sweated out her first night on top of a sleeping bag, handed over silently and without expression by Rachel G., her sponsor. Rachel had also taped newspapers onto the windows to provide some discretion while still not officially *enabling* by going out and buying the shades that both of them knew Maggie should purchase for herself. But what self? The windows were wide open, begging for breezes anyway, so to hell with decorum. There was no shower curtain.

Maggie took a chaotic shower, stepped out into the puddles, dried herself with dirty laundry, and put on the clean clothes Rachel had laid out in preparation for this important day. Hair still wet, she walked outside onto the same block where she had lived for fifteen years in an entirely different reality, in a different apartment with another person and, eventually, their child. When it finally became time for her discharge from institutional control, she had been unable to decide anything including where she wanted to live *now*, and could not imagine *how* to know. And when this insanely overpriced, unimpressive box was suddenly available through a friend of Rachel's, on that very same street, it became the easiest thing to do. The friend was nice, put the phone and lease in Maggie's name. Everyone owed Rachel a favor for someone else. Return. No decisions. Same subway stop, same corner crosswalk, and the very same deli to stumble to in the mornings. Only, the stumble of sobriety is like an empty farm in August, too many flies, the quiet heat, and the pressure of nature holding its breath. It is old for the world, and yet for Maggie it was new.

"Welcome back." This was Nick Stammas, owner of Nick's Deli. A forgotten piece of furniture in Maggie's life. "I haven't seen you in so long."

Does he know?

"Yeah. Hi, Nick. What's new?"

"We got a new deli guy. This is Joe. He just came here from Albania."

A skinny, disoriented young man with a crooked smile, and a five o'clock shadow at eight o'clock in the morning, smiled and waved and looked confused.

"He don't speak English yet. Look." He pointed with his chin across the street to something she could barely discern. "You know what they got? Something called cold-pressed juice. Ten dollars. They have *scones*, made with cheese. Four dollars. Iced soy lattes. A pastry, coffee, and juice and you have to hand over a twenty. If you need soy, why do you buy cheese? I'm telling you . . ."

"Crazy."

"And I'm telling you." He leaned in from the chest. "It's a *chain*. Forget it! How ya doin'?" The kernel of real concern gave it all away.

Everyone knows.

"Good."

"That's great news." He smiled. He was warm and beefy and hairy and overworked. Talking to customers enriched his life, a window into the soul of a microcosm of the world.

"Thanks, Nick. How are you?"

"Can't complain, the kids, you know. How long has it been?"

How long *has* it been?

"Since before the election."

"Oh my God, Maggie. Forget about it. Don't even talk about it. What can you say? Don't make yourself crazy."

For the foreseeable future, Nick would be the first person she would speak to every morning. He would be her family, her man. She wanted to respond warmly to his recognition. The truth is that Maggie wanted to love Nick Stammas, and standing at the corner between the overpriced mints, tasteless bananas, and packages of dried-out, sugary Danish, she tried to open her heart, to feel good about him. To decide to be happy, *no matter what*. But once again the comfort she yearned for just was not there. Instead of an old friend, she found a kind of looming clown. He was, after all, a bored person playing a role, trapped in service to people like her. That neighborhood guy. She, too, had a role. What was it again? To buy things from him, give him something to tell his wife, TV in the background. "That lady was back in this morning, the fuckup. Her skin is sour." Was that the meaning of Maggie Terry's life?

"Eighteen months."

"You look skinny," he said. "Go to the gym."

Do I go to the gym? She had no idea of who she was.

"Okay."

"Did you see the paper today?"

She panicked. "Did someone bomb something?" What about Alina? Is she safe?

"I tell you, Maggie, I am just as afraid of the president bombing someone who'll bomb us back as I am of some crazy kid. No, no, don't pay attention to that bullshit. Too stressful. Forget politics. I'm talking about the poor girl who got choked." He held up a tabloid, read out the headline, "Actress Strangled." Clucking for the record, Nick folded the paper expertly and set that morning's *New York Post* down on the counter. It was for her. "The usual?"

"What's my usual?"

"Two large black coffees, a packet of Tylenol, and the paper. I have an espresso machine now. You want an espresso?"

Nauseated by living, that menu seemed impossible. Coffee for the shakes; painkiller for someone trying not to feel pain.

"No thanks. I'll take . . . something . . . healthy. Do you have . . ." she grasped, "smoothies?"

Where did that come from?

"Nope," he shook his head sadly.

"Nick, help. What do you have that is good for me?"

He smiled. He didn't shave regularly, this guy. "I'll give you a mint tea and an apple. How's that?"

"Sure."

"It's good for your heart. And Maggie, do some aerobics, Pilates, something!"

Behind the counter were rows of cigarettes, $17 a pack. They no longer looked necessary. Maybe she was getting better. Why would anyone buy those dangerous things? Who are the people who still could? The immune! That's who. Now that she had crossed over into the category of the wounded, there was no going back.

Another "reason" that Maggie returned to the same old street where she had lived stoned and blasted out of her mind for fifteen out of the thirty years that she'd been using was that Mike Fitzgerald's law firm was only a five-block walk from her new apartment. Maybe it was princessy, but she didn't think she could handle the subway at rush hour, and she certainly couldn't pay for a cab. Handle. Of course, she could *handle* the subway. What kind of bullshit crap excuse was that? She could walk down those scum-and-gum-encrusted stairs, stand anxiously in the heat and ice. She could hang on to slimy poles, smash into clueless tourists forever, or sit face front into some man's crotch. But it would make things harder. The sweating, the standing, the fear of offending the wrong person, clutching her purse, checking out the undercovers, trying not to look paranoid, watching the vermin square-dancing across the platform, men handling their own genitals like they were tough tomatoes in fragile skins.

Frances had long fled the neighborhood so there was

no chance of Maggie being mistaken for a *stalker*. That word used to mean men who chased movie stars with guns or stabbed their ex-girlfriends and ex-wives. Now it could be used to mean a trembling shadow hovering over her own girlfriend, her ex-girlfriend, and their own . . . own . . . child. They were gone, and Maggie had returned here to the abandoned desert reeking of their absence. There was revulsion as she tried to push back that image of herself, drinking in a bar, doing lines with idiots, while Alina was being born. Knowing that she had to get her ass to the hospital, that Frances was expecting her to . . . be there. Now she could see that she was just a frightened little child herself, afraid of facing facts—that Frances was going to have someone to love more than she had ever loved Maggie. And that this was a repetition. A pattern. Always being the person who wasn't loved as much, enough, or at all. That kid was going to take all of that away from her, being precious to another person, to Frances. So, fuck that. She did another line. She knows now that was . . . wrong, no other word for it: *wrong*. And she apologized even back then. She said she was sorry and she meant it, but it was *such* a bad move. No one wanted to hear the reason why.

But here she was now, sober, and it had been years ago, really. Some things get better over time and some things have to be made better. Some improvement is a group endeavor . . . or forgiveness and understanding and listening. And thank God for Mike Fitzgerald; God bless him. And there was no God. And she would not say "Higher Power bless him" because there was a level of profanity in that robotic recitation of imposed vocabulary. But thanks to Mike, and his mercy, she was coming out of rehab to a job that wasn't demeaning and provided the chance to prove herself so that she could get Alina back, the only reason to prove anything. At least shared custody. That shouldn't be in the realm of the impossible if she did what she was told. At least *visitation.*

"Let me help you out," Mike said on Family Day. The social worker thought Mike was her dad but he wasn't old enough. It was the kindness, the soft soulful eyes that everyone wanted their father to have. Mike's surprise job offer two weeks later provided opportunity where there might have been only a wave goodbye. He's a blessing, that guy. Professor Mike. He'd given her an A back, back, back in grad school, and that had made her entire career possible. Everyone had been telling her to go to law school, but somehow—she was only realizing this now, in fact Maggie was only realizing everything now—she couldn't picture herself being a lawyer and doing the kind of drugs she wanted to do. It was unconscious, like everything else, but fucking present. Her father drank constantly and he was a rich man. She could have done the same, but then she would be surrounded by the type of people she grew up with: rich drunks. What would be wrong with that? Maggie crossed Eighth Avenue and looked in the window of an abandoned storefront. What was going in there? A cookie place? Who buys all those cookies and macaroons and macarons and gelatos and macro, ultrasweet coffees with pumps of flavored sugar and whipped cream? Stoned people.

She looked at herself, reflected in the empty glass,

untouched tea in one hand, apple in the other. She didn't want a cigarette and she didn't want a five-dollar cookie. So, something must be getting better. And then, this *idea* came into her heart, like a drill through the ear, or an endoscopic camera sent down to photograph her gut, or a punch in the jaw, or a terrible pain, or a failure, like a storm, or a false accusation, or a mistake that never should have happened, or the bullet through . . . an idea, that's all. The kind of thought that can only occur when a person is no longer stoned entered into her vocabulary of herself. Maggie realized that she didn't want to go to law school because everyone in that world of rules and domination and justifying systems and *order* would see who she really was. Right away. She would be familiar. Her disaster would be like their mother's breakdown or their neighbors teetering around the country club. She wanted privacy for her disaster, so she put herself in a world where no one could read her blatant code. That was the *real* reason that she'd wanted to join the police force. To hide. And Mike Fitzgerald was the only voice out there telling her to "give it a try."

She liked the culture of the cops, that was the truth. There was a weird vulnerability that came from being afraid of everyone, having contempt for them, and trying to help them while also controlling them and wanting their love. It worked for her. She hid her shame in the bullying lack of pretension, and she wouldn't have to compete. She came onto the force with her advanced degrees, and loved being one of the guys and how forgiving they were . . . to each other. Okay, it could not have gone worse in the end, but for a while it was a fair ride. It did destroy her life, but she still had one. Now Mike was giving her a second, second chance, this time at surviving. He wasn't blaming her and he wasn't blaming himself. That was his miracle. And this time, survival had to take.

CHAPTER TWO

9:00 AM

Maggie made it to the lobby of Mike's office building with this new information buoying some kind of . . . could it be actual *optimism*? Too bad her entire aware- ness of herself had to be retrospective. It would have been easier to learn as you go, not after it's all over. But, here she was. The Program tells us to be in the present, but Maggie's past was still at the wheel. She was supposed to create a new "now" to replace the old one, and starting this job was a step in . . . well, a start.

Advice comes from surprising corners, and Nick had told her to do Pilates. She didn't know what Pilates was, exactly, but the word *aerobics* came out of some ancient memory, helping her eschew the crowded ele- vators, opting to jog . . . or something up the stairs. It was all part of the new start! Okay, let's go.

Maggie had always been what the world consid- ered a good-looker, a WASP queen who'd gotten too many bonus points for being blond and leggy. She had a great body and didn't need to live in a gym. But lots of pretty, blond girls are miserable. No one feels sorry for them, and why should they? Only 2 percent of the world is actually blond. The rest are reaching for a mask or a crown. When Maggie's mother killed herself, the housekeeper made her put on her prettiest dress for the funeral, and everyone told her how beautiful she looked. What a stupid thing to say to a little girl whose mother had left her behind: "You're so pretty." All that really meant was "Let's not talk about anything because you have the right color hair." So, nobody cared when her father let her have a highball. And that's why she got away with so much at work because the New York City Police Department is filled with brunettes. Even the most racist of the old-school, grandfathered-in, third-generation officers are darker than they want to admit. And as sick to death as people are of that white monster, *blond* has the power of the Abominable Snowman. The whiteness staggers from a distance and tramples cities with its roar.

Now exhausted, only at the second floor, slumped in her phony gesture toward exercise and a better life, Maggie was confused. She supposedly could pull it together and pull it off, so why wasn't she? There were tricks to hide behind: hair, face, lips. These were effective masks, but she wanted to be real. Right? To be . . . what did they call it? Her*self.*

Then, in the ultimate failure of this new tiny moment of opportunity, she sloshed tea onto her clean shirt. Stunned in the stairwell, looking down at the stain spreading across her breasts, she quickly abandoned all of the hopes and expectations Rachel's preparations had offered: that, for once, Maggie might both act and look appropriate. She gave up at the third landing and stopped to wait for the elevator panting and stained. She had made a spectacle of herself already. And nothing had even happened.

The elevator arrived, and there, confronting Maggie's entry into the fluorescent box, was a small child, the same cruel glory of other people that stood around every bend and its apex of assault. She tried to look away, staring instead at her own reflection in the metallic door. Sick of her endless problems, she finally let her eyes land, ravenously, on the seven-year-old girl holding her mother's hand. She knew the pleasure in that—when Alina was so small, and that tiny, wrinkle-free, fat little paw reached for her own, naturally, wanting to touch her. Expecting Maggie's love just by being there. It was magic, those moments. The assumptions.

This breech is what set Maggie apart from humanity and put her in the animal category, the state's disavowal of her acquired feelings of motherhood. No, wrong. Animals are not kept from their children. Perhaps maggots don't watch their offspring grow up, or bedbugs. But cockroaches are dutiful mothers; they nurture their young by self-destructing, not like Maggie, who'd never nurtured. She'd seen cockroach mothers' bodies dissolve into crackly shells as the tiny new black ones scattered, so small, their heads not yet protruding. Sure, she'd started out awful, but pretty quickly she liked, loved, and then adored Alina. She wanted her. She wanted her friendship; Frances knew that. And yes, Maggie was getting high in the bathroom before work. Everyone understands that now. But disease doesn't cancel out bonds. Her heart was breaking, right there in the elevator. Longing. The absence of Alina was her scarlet letter, and it was scrawled in the desire she felt whenever custodial parents paraded in the streets, flaunting their indifference and their privileged right to not celebrate daily for their good fortune. Anyway, luck had a lot to do with it. They don't say that in Program but everyone knows it's a fact. One person dies and the other lives to recover. The lucky ones live.

"She's beautiful," Maggie finally cooed strategically to the elevator mother, though she wanted to sweep the small one in her arms and bury her nose in the child's sweaty little neck and tell her the truth, that she was beautiful. But it is not permitted to open one's heart to someone else's child. "I have a little girl, too."

And then, having paid the penance, it was finally reasonable to face the pretty one directly, look into those unknowing eyes.

"Just your age."

Maggie had been sober for eighteen months. That should mean something to Frances. It should.

The elevator surprised her by stopping at six and the mother and child stepped off. Again, the absence was palpable, and underlying that, Maggie had only noticed her own destination, not theirs, because she was still selfish, after all. Still so self-involved with her pain that she had no room for anyone else's. It was all about her. It was all about her spacey inability to focus, her head filled with cotton, her lack of recognition of what was before her and within her. Me, me, me. Her whining, her self-blame that obscured every other living thing, the mirror that she thought was a window. It was all about poor, poor Maggie, who finally chomped down on the apple and ate it through. Stepping out of the elevators to face the office door of FITZGERALD & ROBBINS, ATTORNEYS AT LAW. There was no place to throw the core so she ate that too. And only then did she ring the bell.

"Good morning," the intercom sang. Someone was cheery.

"Hi, it's Maggie Terry. I'm here for my first day."

Overshare.

There was a slightly discernable commotion on the other end, and a bit of hesitation behind the door, just enough to unnerve her. And then it opened, unveiling the entire staff of Fitzgerald & Robbins, standing nervously beneath a banner screaming WELCOME MAGGIE, which was pure Michael—all good intentions. But the sign was as droopy as their enthusiasm, like a highly paid magician at the birthday party of a girl who knows that no one loves her.

"Welcome," they recited discordantly.

Michael wheeled himself before the hesitant staff and made a show of warmly taking her hand.

"Welcome, Maggie. We are so glad that you are here."

He's the same. She'd barely noticed his charismatic will when he'd come to see her in rehab. It was so embarrassing that it had come to institutionalization. And all the trouble he'd gone through to make the visit. Her primary response to his kindness was to be upset with herself and swat away the concern, eyes down, not even knowing how to fake it. But here she was, *better*, pulled together except for a big greenish stain on her blouse, but able to look him in the eye and act—as they say in Program *as if*—as if it were all somehow okay. He was still handsome, much grayer since the shooting, but in tip-top shape due to personal training and suits impeccably tailored for a man in a wheelchair. No bunches at the crotch, no sloppy shoulders, that too-large gold wedding band still bragging from his tanned left hand.

"Thank you." She tried to be confident but it came out like a whimper. "I'm so happy . . . I mean . . ." She was sweating. She wiped her forehead on her sleeve.

Michael survived his life by being obliviously joyful at the most opportune moments. It was his strength and his downfall. He was doing the right thing and he was happy with himself, and since he was happy with himself, he was doing the right thing. Again.

"I've told the staff all about you." He beamed, waved back his magic wand of a hand, and revealed the molted faces of unease that constituted Mike's trusted team. These were the people she had to befriend and then join in with, heart and soul.

Maggie saw the worry on their faces, how they imagined the worst. How many other cockamamie schemes had Michael subjected them to over the years? All with equal insistence and oom-pa-pa. Would she be his next disaster? They were taking bets. These folks had been made gun-shy by all the failed experiments and high-risk recklessness in the life of someone who always believed others could do what he could. *Recover*. Well, they couldn't. Mike may have been Teflon, but his beleaguered staff was certainly scratched.

"I bragged about you." He was still smiling. How can he still be smiling? Doesn't he realize that this is obviously all a terrible mistake? "Just yesterday, about the brilliant thesis you wrote under my supervision at Columbia." He was still holding her hand, like Santa. "About solving crimes without technology. Relying on compassion!" His gray eyes watered; he was so moved by her *compassion*, her brilliance, her human flaw, and the inevitable redemption in which he would be a key player. "Maggie dear, you understand the desperate mind."

"It takes one to know one."

Mike laughed. Like she was funny. Like she was warm, charming, on the ball. Like she was him instead of herself.

"Ahem."

Maggie looked up and saw Enid Robbins, Michael's junior partner, scowling; she was so good at it, maybe that was just her role. Maybe she didn't hate Maggie at first sight, *maybe*. Enid just couldn't help herself. It was a wish, that everything would straighten itself out and the warm embrace of an understanding world would manifest before her, this very first day of . . . the rest of the day. But no, unfortunately Enid was clearing her throat to exhibit protest of the most vehement sort. Maggie dropped her fantasizing and took in the real message immediately: Enid didn't like this arrangement one bit. Enid wanted it to be clear that she was being forced to go along with a rescue mission that seemed pointless and time-consuming. At least fifty-five, Maggie estimated, and Enid could not believe she was still doing things that she did not want to do. Why? The whole room watched her ask herself. Why? Why? It screamed disbelief that full autonomy had still not arrived in her life of always wanting just that. What went wrong?

"And the tough courageous way," Michael continued, unstoppable. "That you, Maggie, tried to save the life of my son." He turned away from her to face his staff with the hard facts. "This woman has guts."

"Michael." Enid practiced no restraint. "That was not *your* fault."

Ah! So now Maggie understood the terms. Three years before, she'd woken up from a nod in a shithole and, instead of just rolling over, had found the strength to take a cab to Michael's apartment, making him come downstairs and pay the fare. It was eight o'clock in the morning. Looking like the hell in which she had been dying and indifferently smelling like neglect, she'd explained carefully to Michael that his oldest boy, Alex, was copping dope.

"I can't tell you how I know," she said. "But it's true."

"That's impossible."

Michael didn't feel there was enough evidence. He doubted this report.

"I know he's a bit . . . immature . . . but, he'll grow out of it on his own time. And I am here for him for as long as it takes."

"What does *here for him* mean, Michael?" She was angry. "Doing nothing?"

Michael was insulted in his hubris. No one talks to him like that. "I love my son and I am letting him find his way."

"He has a disease," she cried. It was all about herself. She wasn't going out of her way to prostrate herself for someone else's kid—it was for her own soul. Please, please help me. If he would help his own son, maybe he could help her, too. "You are his father!"

Where was her father? Why was he standing by and letting her destroy her second family the way he had destroyed her first? Why wasn't her father racing over in a cab to swoop her up in his arms and apologize so that she could stop getting high and love Frances and Alina? Why wasn't her father sitting down with Frances and planning the intervention that would show, finally, that someone loved her? Why was she so alone in this?

"Mike, you have to do something. You have to act!"

There was a viciousness then, never before surfaced, that crawled over Mike's very white teeth and gripped control of his face, filling it with the startling rage of being defended. The venom of self-righteous denial.

"Don't tell me how to be a father. I love my son no matter what."

"Then do something." Love is an action, not a feeling, she wanted to add but suddenly felt exhausted. She needed to take a shower and get ready for work at the station and she was wasting her time telling Mike the truth, and he was blaming the telling instead of the horrible facts themselves.

"You're a mess," he said. "You're disorganized."

"So what, I'm still helping you."

That was why getting sober had seemed so impossible. The truth was supposed to be a gift, but nobody wanted to hold it. Being high was a lie, but there was only one replacement, a reality that no one else wanted to share. Frances was the same way. She claimed she wanted Maggie to stop using but they both knew that, for a long time, this wasn't true. An equal is a mirror after all. So, with two years of infant care under their belts, and the joy of a real child with a point of view, Frances found a cute young girl who was willing to let her run the ship. Keeping Maggie sick made it all easier and excusable. There was someone to blame, and so the disease served everyone's needs. And that dirty, sad morning it had handed Mike his life's biggest excuse.

Now, *clean*, standing in his office, squeezed by Mike's big fat welcome of regret, Maggie remembered his face when he had dismissed her stinking news about the demise of his son. Was it simply because he didn't have the *guts* to be the hero he'd always pretended to be? To face facts? Of course that was why. He loved his self-conception more than he loved anyone else. And if his son was a fuckup, a depressed, life-wasting drug addict, then Mike wasn't perfect and that could never, ever be. Now, years and tragedies later, his son was dead. And some substitute had to be redeemed.

And so, Maggie now stood, miraculously employed. Now, she was the hero and Mike was to blame. Everyone has to have a hero.

"Maggie has *guts*," Mike repeated. "She had the guts to approach me, and I didn't have the gumption to listen."

Still holding her hand, Mike wheeled himself to Enid, taking hers as well, and linking the women through his own human chain.

"Enid has a great talent, Maggie, like yours. She is a fighter. She was on the board of Hillary's campaign in New York State. She was there, in the hotel ballroom, when Hillary had to—"

"Concede to the Orange Monster." Enid was still mad.

"Yes, thank you. Enid knows how to fight, and she knows how to survive. And she is raising money for Democrats as we speak because she never gives up. Isn't that right, Enid?"

"I won't be happy until I see them all led away in handcuffs."

"That a girl, Enid. And I believe you will ultimately triumph."

"Well." Enid would not smile. "None of us know what is going to happen. Those Republicans are so evil. They will do everything they can to rob the national treasury; they are so greedy . . ." She had to stop herself.

"Maggie, Enid raised four children before acing law school. Can you imagine?"

Maggie felt the truth of her own failure. She'd lost one to custody.

"Enid," she said. "Thank you so much for this oppor—"

"Don't thank me." Enid had a china-teacup quality to her skin. Pale blue stretched over fragile bones. She either could have been imported from England or righteous American high society from a small town in Texas. "I was married to a compulsive gambler, and I don't believe in giving people third chances. Michael forced this absurd plan on us by charming me into a coma."

"I'm sorry," Maggie stumbled. "I didn't mean to thank you."

"Time will tell." Enid wasn't nasty, per se. She just left no room for doubt, the harshest of options. "We'll see."

"And this . . ." Michael smiled, pointing to a short, burdened, overweight black man in his early thirties who was staring at his phone, clearly needing to be anywhere else because he had so many things on his plate, things that mattered like his clients, his wife, his co-op board, his annoying mother, his overachieving sister, his Dominican personal trainer recommended by Michael. "This is Craig Williams, your coinvestigator."

Craig looked up and smiled, a Harvard or Yale kind of smile, like he was happy to see her but wanted to be sure she knew he really wasn't.

"Craig is our IT whiz."

Once the smile was completed Craig went back to his device, so when Maggie reached out her hand and said hi, he missed it and left her arm suspended in optimistic traction.

"Great to meet you," Maggie tried again, too hard, instead of taking the huge hint of rejection, and she regretted it because it was pushy to try to connect. And it became insistent and inherently criticizing to tell Craig, in front of everyone, that he should be looking at her and shaking her hand instead of solving crime.

The pause in the room's chatter loomed into an intrusive silence. Used to everyone else's banter as white noise, Craig sensed that something was wrong and finally looked up. He smiled that $250,000-tuition smile and in a charming, friendly, and almost loving way clarified his position.

"I don't really need a coinvestigator. Frankly, I think it's insulting."

Maggie shook hands with the air.

"I'm Sandy," a voice called forth, the receptionist trying to assert herself. It was an office filled with resentment, like all families.

And Sandy smiled at Mike for confirmation that she mattered, and he smiled back, and Maggie understood that the anger in this room was not directed at the daddy in the wheelchair who signed their paychecks, but at each other. Because that is what daddies do all day. They breed division between others so they can stay on top.

Maggie still thought like a detective, even if she could hardly dress herself. It was some kind of interim personality, in transition from one life to another, clinging to the core instinct of *investigation*. Instead of the freedom of authority, she had to develop routine. But she still thought analytically. Maggie could be staggering into a Narcotics Anonymous meeting and still suss out every room like it was a crime scene, and in some way, it usually was. She cataloged the personalities: Enid, the brittle detractor; Craig, the well-trained but suffering resistor; and now bouncy, ditzy, and frazzled Sandy, dressed in one of her three professional blouses, who leaped up and hugged Maggie, unable to resist gratitude for anyone else who would surely be on the outs here in the office, as she, Sandy, the lowly servant, always was and always would be.

"WELCOME, Maggie! Welcome!"

Maggie understood by Sandy's *weirdness* and *wrongness* that she must be another one of Mike's charity cases. Perhaps she was a failed actress, or soon-to-be failed actress, unless by chance she got cast at the last minute as the frazzled ditzy one on a sitcom about an office, and could finally buy that one bedroom with an elevator.

"Hi, Sandy. Thanks."

"Every morning when you come into work, Maggie, well, I'll be right here. And I'll buzz you in." She sat down abruptly behind her front desk, content at having asserted her role, and so the initiation hazing seemed to have come to an end.

"See," Michael grinned at the obvious success of his plan, "everything is going to be just fine."

CHAPTER THREE

NOON

By midmorning she was already itchy. By quarter to twelve, concentration had become impossible. Two hours of staring at the Fitzgerald & Robbins employee handbook's list of procedures, interspersed with Mike's witty catchphrases, produced no new understanding of her fate. Revelation was all she was looking for, apparently, and the other daily requirements of being normal and functional sat in the way of her transformation into a person happy enough to not be a burden to others. But rules were rules, so Maggie hoped she could pick up what she needed to know on the job. Winging it was both her secret strength and fatal flaw.

By the time church bells announced noon's arrival, she strategically waited two full minutes and then ran down the stairs and hurried the three blocks to the local YMCA. Rachel had made a map of all the 12 Step meetings in a ten-block radius, which was probably a violation of Rachel's Al-Anon requirement: Don't Be a Doormat; Don't Be a Nag. But Maggie was grateful. She never would have made it through the day without support, and she never would have been able to think clearly enough to have figured out a list in advance of the moment of truth. Need was always a crisis and crisis always a surprise. There were a lot of meetings in Chelsea, the West Village, and Midtown: debtors, meth heads, gamblers, purgers, people who were not loved and therefore loved others to a degree that someone deemed "too much." Maggie's lunch break was spent eating her nails at an NA meeting in the Y's gray-carpeted rear room. Despite qualifying for many branches of Program, she knew what *itchy* meant. It meant she was an addict and had to get her sorry ass to NA.

It didn't take long, feeling ill at ease in her normally familiar folding chair, to realize that this meeting was the first time she'd entered the Rooms as an employed person. The difference was immediately obvious. Her uncomfortable work clothes made her standard fall-back, slouching, impossible. No longer able to huddle against the force of her own self-created misfortune, she had to sit upright, legs crossed at the ankles. Fear of wrinkles, and even more stains, dictated her posture. This made it harder for Maggie to feel. Fear usually did that job. Refusing to collapse took a resolve that interfered with pain, making it secondary to the effort of sitting up. Was there still only room for one thing at a time in her broken-down machine of a body? Either pain or maintenance? Pain or posture? This was not the goal. The goal was integration, to have it *all*—pain, posture, clean shirts, nuanced thoughts, clarity. Alina within arm's reach. A self, a self. She had none of that, but today, for the first time since she had been stripped of her badge in disgrace, she had a job. Gratitude!

One Step at a Time. She inhaled, relaxed, actually smiled. Her heart opened, and then, suddenly, the pain came roaring in: the smell of her daughter's waxy ear as she gently cleaned it with a Q-tip, the ultimate sign of domesticity. Was it always going to be this way? As soon as some space was cleared in her mental fog, the loss of her beautiful Alina's giggle would intrude on that nanosecond of self-satisfaction. How could it be that all this work of trying to be a real person was only to make room for the pain? It was exhausting. To not fight it off, but to learn to sit with it. To face it. This was not how she had imagined *progress*. Progress was resolution and happiness. Alina smelled of clean dirt, because her heart was clean.

As the meeting's qualifier rambled on, Maggie picked up the phrase "Our household was always in chaos." Of course that was a claim Alina could already make as she approached the age of six. Chaos. No point in Maggie denying that her child's life already bore the consequences of her own epic failure. Alina would always hold the yelling, the missed appointments, the crazy-high acting out, and then Maggie's disappearance into rehab and her ban, her end. Did Alina even remember her anymore?

A glimmer of a memory of a moment with Alina tried to crawl into Maggie's mind, but she stopped it. Alina toddling over to her, propelled by the uncontrollable, newly minted ability to walk, hands waving for balance, her smile so huge. Some teeth. Maggie. Her daughter called her *Maggie*. She'd heard Frances say it so many times: Maggie, stop it. Maggie, calm down. Maggie, honey, relax. That doesn't make any sense, Maggie. Maggie, please. Maggie sounded like Mommy, right? *Right?*

Oh God, someone at the meeting was sharing about Trump.

"He's everywhere, terrorizing the people," a young woman was saying. This was not the place to talk about the president. Maggie wanted her to shut up. Deal with it yourself.

Maggie knew that once she started collecting Alina moments, they would become limited and dried up, repetitive because there was never going to be a new experience with her beloved child. Not ever. Unless . . . unless . . . well, what's-her-name, Frances's new wife—actually her first legal wife—would have to die or shoot heroin or something and that could always happen. After all, humans are unpredictable, and vulnerability is the definition of being alive. But . . . but, that was a lot to ask for, that Frances would find another addict, a disaster on the other end. New wife *Maritza* worked in Administration. They tended to be a bit more sober, office workers. Lots of people do repeat though, substituting one fucked-up addict lover for the next. If there was an addict at her office, Frances would have had a good chance of finding her. Maggie could hope for that much. Then she wouldn't have to be the only terrible person in Frances's life. Maybe if it happened a second time, Frances would have to take some of the blame.

Some woman, Elvira, was sharing her story. She

looked washed-up. She was one of those addicts whose jaw muscles had slackened and her teeth were whittled down and on their way out. She'd overdone it. She was talking about how, when she was a kid, someone had blamed her for everything wrong in the world while she was sucking his cock, or some such common addict-as-child situation. In response, she'd spent decades trying to get back at him by jabbing her arms, hitting the pipe, and selling hand jobs, and it was just too fucking late.

"No one ever called the police on my father." She had the growl of a smoker, and the vocabulary of someone who lived in 12 Step meetings and prison-mandated therapy. She had memorized what the social workers had told her and recited it. Sometimes twice a day. "Since no one had ever called the police on my father, I was always calling the police on anyone I couldn't control. Then I found out the hard way that I couldn't control the police, and ended up in Bayview and then I went to Bedford."

It was admirable, though, Maggie had to admit, to come crawling to meetings when it was too fucking late. But then again, where else was this chick going to go? And people always have to go somewhere. This girl wore her history on her face, which meant no going back to normalcy. Her whole life was over. She would never be able to pass. May as well sit here where the wealthy gay men and Xanaxed housewife types would be forced to listen. Nobody else was going to pay attention to this one, unless they were high or behind bars.

It was a type.

That other lady over there, who was now speaking,

Sandra. She was one who had quietly given up exactly the way Maggie expected to give up. And as they say in Program, Maggie *identified.* In her, Maggie saw her own negative potential and likely future self. Sandra came to NA meetings because she could only watch television so many hours a day. This woman was in too much pain to sit through a movie, she couldn't bear another meal alone, she couldn't walk down a street because she couldn't see something that mattered and have no one to tell it to. So, she went to NA meetings, thirty years after her last dose. Her sobriety wasn't threatened, but it was all she had left, NA. She was revisiting, revisiting it all over and over again, those mistakes. The mistakes of her life. The things that no one would forgive her for, even if they could no longer remember exactly what she had done. This was Maggie's fate, clearly. As long as Alina was kept from her, she was fated to dead time. And tasteless apples. Maybe she should buy a TV to help pass the rest of her sentence, her life. Do they still have TV stores, she wondered, with salesmen who explain how everything works? Or did she have to buy a computer and learn how to go online so she could order one? How did that work again?

"Is there anything ever on TV besides Senate hearings and a media obsessed with being dissed by a president no one can understand how to get rid of?" A Jewish lady was complaining. Must be a teacher.

Serenity Prayer already. Stand and touch another human's hand, maybe the only flesh in your life. "Keep coming back, it works if you work it, so work it, you're worth it."

What the hell did that even mean? Spend her whole life in the repetition of meetings so she didn't die in the repetition of picking up? Why couldn't Frances see that the lack of access to her own child kept Maggie in circles of despair? Maybe that's what Frances wanted, to punish Maggie so hard and so constantly that *she* would never have to take anything on herself. Asshole. Frances had what everyone wanted. Why be such a bitch? What is she fucking getting out of it? Frances! *Frances!* As long as Maggie couldn't be a full person— love, deal, connect authentically—then Frances was perfect. Maggie's loneliness was evidence of Frances's success. The NA meeting was over, so why was she still thinking?

The room had emptied, and Maggie picked up her purse. Stopping in the ladies' room, she looked in the mirror. No wrinkles. Okay, that was an accomplishment. Her life was a dead horse but there were no wrinkles. Right on! The miracle of the 12 Steps. And now she had a job. That too was good. Gratitude. It was great.

CHAPTER FOUR

1:30 PM

That afternoon was Maggie's first staff meeting. She had been warned by a gentle, whispery Sandy that there was a signal, a series of buzzes, that meant *right now!* Toilet paper in hand, needle in arm, cock in mouth, or one foot out the window, when summoned, everything had to stop for the gathering of the team. BLAST BLAST BLAST. Maggie jumped and ran to the conference room, the first to arrive. The room itself was a brand. It trumpeted how Enid and Mike wanted to be perceived: sophisticated, smart, in control, and perfectly situated. But no matter how high-end the art design, every system has flaws. Showing the flaws is what makes life . . . real? Work? Bearable? Possible.

That's what her NYPD partner Julio Figueroa had always said, "Some people care more about their image than anything." And his example shifted as the years passed, but the final one, Maggie remembered, was

Beyoncé. "Take Beyoncé," Julio would say. "She has enough money. She *still* cares what we think about her." And this belief proved very effective when they were on a case, sussing out who to believe, who was invested, who would benefit, who was just out of control. "Some people only care about others." Julio always pointed that out when they were investigating a new case. "Remember," he'd say. "There is always history to every relationship, and history is filled with a lack of resolution."

She waited quietly, staring out through the impressive glass wall of the spacious office onto the valley of rooftop penthouses, hidden behind landscaped greenery so extravagant that there appeared to be actual watermelons, corn stalks, and apple trees growing out of the heads of buildings. Urban grow-your-own. She had missed this trend and so many others. She had missed the return of bacon, she had missed young men with hair buns caring about how coffee beans were roasted, she had missed apps, of course, and expensive green water. She'd missed *Minecraft* and could not ID a single celebrity in *People* magazine. She'd been drunk through all of it, and then she had been in court and in detox and in rehab and in a bathrobe and slippers, crying, tearing her heart out over the mess she had made, and in this way, she had missed voting. And there were hearings on every television in every restaurant window and taxi radio, and outlandish headlines on every newsstand. The level of blatant lying by the president was remarkable. Observing it had become a national pastime, like bird watching. He made a bunch of addicts look reasonable. Trump was giving people approval for being ignorant, and too many of them seemed to love him for it. She'd been a detective long enough to know why people liked bullies; it's because they wanted to be bullies but weren't powerful enough to pull it off. That's the nature of submission.

One time Maggie and Julio had been called in to deal with a domestic. When they arrived, a family—a father, mother, and young son—were crawling around naked on the floor of their apartment. They thought they were lions. They growled and roared and ate raw meat with their hands. Later, when the shrinks separated them, it turned out that only the father was truly psychotic. The other two were only imitating him. They identified with him so strongly out of fear, that they entered his insanity and took it on. That was like America: imitation as degradation, as a desperate grasp for survival.

She looked up. Craig had joined her, immersed in his machine.

"How do they farm up there?" she whispered to Craig, busy performing *busy*.

"Low-maintenance, subirrigated planter systems."

Maggie suddenly thought of flowers and wondered if she could keep anything alive. She thought about someday after work buying flowers, whose deaths were guaranteed, but they would need to go in something. There was a time when people bought coffee in cans and then used them to sprout avocado seeds, but that was when she was still an undergraduate living in a Vassar dorm and made her own coffee and added Kool-Aid to grain alcohol and shopped for avocados. Now that staying sober was a full-time job, the thought of all those tasks and responsibilities overwhelmed her. She would conserve in other arenas: live off take-out and delivery, never open a can or prepare a dish. But if she could keep a plant alive, that might be a good thing.

"Can I grow tomatoes in a studio apartment?" she asked Craig, only realizing by his expression of negation that she had sealed her fate with the words *studio apartment*. Of course, he didn't answer, which was an act of compassion in itself, really. It relieved her from more recognition of how much she wasn't ready to be on this job.

Mike and Enid entered the conference room with a joyful radiance, making clear that this office was a *happy* place. It was designed to be described as "filled with life." Photos of the good old times covered the walls. There was evidence of important friends and impressive handshakes, grateful, good-looking families living it up. Portraits smiled down on the room: Enid and Mike with Hillary Clinton, Mike with Bill, photos of his dead son Alex, as though there was nothing to hide. Screaming pictures of Mike running, before he was felled by a sore loser's bullet. Mike playing touch football, and later post-rehab shots of him playing wheelchair polo and winning second place in the local paramarathon, senior division. *I'm alive*, his office wall insisted. *You can't stop me.* It was his kitsch, his shtick, how alive he was. But Mike's son was dead forever, and Maggie knew—better than anyone in that room—that that meant Mike was also dead. That he had to live with having ignored the warnings. That could have . . . could have . . . made a . . . made a . . . difference.

She did remember Mike Fitzgerald telling her that his son was innocent. Sons are always innocent. They get away with everything, but they also never get real help. They self-destruct like Alex did, overdosing in the men's room in Columbia University's Butler Library. Or like the son of her veteran detective partner, Eddie Figueroa: hot-headed or lazy or over-the-top, but still taking the life of a man named Nelson Ashford just because he was looking for his keys.

"It could have been a gun, and then Eddie would be dead. That's what no one wants to understand," Julio wept. "He's innocent. My son."

When Maggie had shown up at Mike Fitzgerald's door, dirty and strung out that very significant morning, he had made a deadly mistake. A narcissistic mistake. He didn't want to acknowledge that his family had problems, normal human conflicts. Addicted kids were so normal that everyone would have understood. But Mike couldn't be like everyone else. He couldn't handle it. He couldn't accept what it meant about him. Underneath all that energy and accomplishment, his upper-crust lifestyle, good standing, and social role, Mike couldn't allow himself to be a person with a child who had a real but normal problem. So, he did nothing. And hence, *apocalypse*. Like Julio, who couldn't have a kid who was a bad cop. He couldn't accept it, just like he never mentioned that his partner, Maggie, was getting high before going out on assignments. That she was drinking in the police car. He never said anything. Julio was good, so nothing around him could go wrong.

But Mike was different, now that his son was dead. Now Mike listened to everything that everyone had to say. He took everyone seriously. He was open now. Now that his son was dead. *Now* he changed, now that it didn't matter.

"Okay, everybody, Maggie, I want you on a case right away."

"Mike." Enid placed her hands on the table. Age spots, of course. "Mike, why don't we start her with something easy? Like a divorce? Not that divorce is easy."

Maggie cringed. She had an enemy already.

Mike shined his light on Enid. He smiled. His eyes were full of his own open heart. He grinned the way women like men to grin. They learn it as boys to make their mothers calm down and let them do what they want. When he was young it telegraphed juicy bastard, and now it said *kind*.

"Now," Michael continued, putting his hairy hand on Enid's spotted one. "We have a high-profile client coming in."

Craig looked up, annoyed. "Who is it? How come nobody tells me anything around here?"

There was a knock on the conference room door.

"Come in!" Mike was beaming now, excited. He knew what was coming.

"Hi," Sandy squeaked, a little more nervous than usual. "She's here!" Sandy giggled.

This indicated to the rest of the staff that she must have recognized the client, which made everyone else even more curious, since Sandy was considered to know nothing about anything that mattered. So, this client had to be someone whose face would be on the kind of TV shows that everyone assumed Sandy watched. "She's here."

"Who's here?" Craig was mad now. "How come I don't know what is going on? Now I'm not prepped. You could have texted me."

Maggie observed it all. She saw Enid's fear, Mike's dominance, Craig's expectation of disrespect, and how no one looked at Sandy at all. No one saw her. And using those same impulses, Maggie noticed that Sandy wore a simple, gorgeous, handmade ring on the middle finger of her right hand. It was rough gold with a garnet stone. It wasn't expensive, but someone had made it for her; it was so perfect for her hand. So, Sandy had people in her life with sophisticated taste who were personal and intelligent and talented. Maggie knew that someone with those kinds of acquaintances, perhaps even friends, had conversations as advanced as their taste in rings. Clocking how none of her new workmates had taken this in, Maggie started to wonder if maybe someday she might be able to get back in the game. She imagined a possibility: gratitude.

"Okay team." Mike straightened his tie like they were going to have the time of their lives. "Here we go."

CHAPTER FIVE

2:00 PM

Lucy Horne was an emblematic person, a weather changer. When she arrived at the party, people felt differently about themselves. They were transformed into those *in the same room as Lucy Horne,* into selfies trying to catch her in the frame. Tweets, profile pics, and status updates galore. Anyone's doubts about their past missteps dissolved into satisfaction, as the revelation of being in a circle that included Lucy Horne was the irrefutable, concrete marker of true success.

"I was a little faggot getting the shit beat out of me in Mississippi, but now I am serving scallop crudo to Lucy Horne."

"I've had nowhere to go on Christmas for sixteen years, but tonight I shook hands with Lucy Horne at a benefit for Planned Parenthood. Who needs love?"

It was the ultimate fuck-you to everyone who had

never believed, who criticized, belittled, shunned, and bullied. It proved that those others were *nothing* and the beleaguered survivor of their hideous status quo was now all.

When Lucy Horne stepped into the conference room at Fitzgerald & Robbins, there was a gasp of silent awe, if silence could gasp. Each party snapped to recognition, then became elevated to their best and most performative self. Mike was *in charge*, Enid was *the voice of reason*, Craig was *dependable and no-nonsense*, Sandy *ready-to-please*. The shroud of negative attention lifted, giving Maggie a breather, a chance to absorb rather than deflect. This unexpected spectacle was her first opportunity to watch her gang of new colleagues respond to something other than her own unwanted presence. Maggie saw Craig glance up at Lucy, have his moment of instant recognition, and then automatically google her. This was the new politesse of the IT professional—no need for business cards, or even introductions. The famous face stimulated the search: websites, Wiki pages, Twitter streams, YouTube channels. Factoids reinforced the faith at the center of the American aesthetic that any person—even with the complications of fame, marketing, and other people's projections—can be summed up.

Lucy had good skin, an expensive body, and healthy hair. She was seductive, smiled with a slight tilt, had excellent, undetectable plastic surgery, and so exemplified "looks great for her age." Sixties looking like fifty. Classy. O'Neill. The false naturalness and natural falsity of a true sophisticate. Aging through the classics. Encompassing the entirety of Chekhov's *The Seagull*:

first playing innocent Nina, then disappointed Masha, and finally the survival-by-narcissism grand dame Irina Arkadina. Maggie's English degree from Vassar always came in handy. There was no loss in being able to reference the Western canon, which peeked around every corner where power lurked.

"Lucy needs no introduction," Mike began. "She was the best student at Yale School of Drama, brought her ethereal gravitas to the New York stage, broke into cinema working with the most credible auteurs; she became the star needed for anything that had meaning, and once she became too big to fail, she herself brought the meaning it lacked of its own accord. She is the brand for quality and for brass: Shakespeare, musicals, new plays, celebrity bios, costume dramas. She even appeared almost nude, once." Everyone laughed. "And then she had a brilliant television career, on *Mister and Mrs.,* for eleven seasons. All along Lucy was carefully allied with the most liberal of causes, birth control, the rights of the poor to something, racism is wrong."

"And Hillary, of course," Enid jumped in.

Maggie noticed everything. She saw Enid smile authentically, which made the whole room unconsciously and silently sigh with relief, like seeing Mama finally happy. Enid seemed to be the group's emotional moderator, and her consent made Mike glow with the joy of successfully being the Leader. That was Enid's function, to withhold approval. And then, when Mike surpassed all bounds, to finally, jarringly, and sparingly deliver. She was one of those tough old ladies who never said "good job" until she meant it, and Mike desperately needed a bullshit detector within arm's length.

Maggie, of course, recognized Lucy, but had only really experienced her as someone to fall asleep to on late-night television. TV was something from Maggie's past life to stare at without comprehension and nod off in front of, something to make the world go away and replace it with nothing, to curl up with Frances and not have to talk. For the stoned, TV was an engaging series of light, graphics, and a wall of too much sound. A stand-in for every missing person and idea, and Lucy Horne was a pillar of this apparatus of mass substitution.

"Mike, thank you so much for seeing me." Lucy telegraphed her emotions of real gratitude, confidence, history of care. Yes, she was an actress, used to the employ of performance to compensate for a cheesy and overwritten improvisational script called *Daily Life*. "I am so . . . grateful." That line was cliché but the delivery was understated balance.

When Maggie worked as a detective all those years, the guys on the force would read the *Post*, and sometimes the *Daily News*, especially if there was a cop story or a sports scandal. In that way, she had become familiar with working-class public figures, corrupt politicians, popes, diplomats caught on dates with topless dancers . . . society's scum, both high and low, and all their many victims. Julio read *El Diario*, but they'd never discussed its contents. Eleven years working with the same partner and she did not share his news. It was a kind of privacy. He didn't know what she was snorting and she didn't know what he was reading.

Julio's in-laws, Julio's nieces and nephews, Julio's father's cancer. Those were the things they discussed. And his son Eddie. How Eddie went down. How to rescue him. And the suspects of course. The human beings under investigation; most of them were guilty: the confused, those with no impulse control, the desperate, the fourteen-year-olds with brains who were doing stupid things because they were so fucking bored, the enraged, the abandoned, the ones who couldn't get anyone to care, the hungry, and most of all, the New Yorkers who didn't know how to solve problems. That was the source of everything bad in the world that wasn't caused by the weather: people not knowing how to solve problems. Detectives know that the truth lies in the order of events. You cannot get at anything's core until you know the order of events. There are initiating actions and then there are consequential ones. Nothing *just* happens, and no one is *just* bad. All detectives know this: people do things for reasons. In order to gather the facts, you have to listen and ask. And if you flash the badge, they are supposed to answer. Murder, child murder, child rape, stealing everything, burning down the house, and, oh yeah, calling the police every time a person can't be bothered to look in the mirror and alter themselves a little. Just a smidge. These were the cases sent to Detectives Terry and Figueroa, over and over again for eleven years. People in trouble.

Maggie suddenly understood, looking at the texture of Lucy Horne's casual/fancy/sporty/singular/stunning/breezy/summer ensemble, that that car, with Julio, had been the safe place where she could hide. How much did Lucy's outfit cost? A thousand dollars? The dirty station houses, the green paint, the lack of comfort, the greasy smell. The holding cells, the bad food, the locker room, the young rookies, the badge. And the squalor in which so many New Yorkers live: cramped quarters, holes in the ceiling, rats de rigueur. Nothing works, not the elevator, not the lights in the stairwell. Not the bathtub, nor the windows. Frances came from a working-class family and when she got mad she'd say that Maggie was slumming, but actually that world was the place to hide in plain sight, away from anyone who couldn't be bothered to see through her. Because, after all, Margaret Elisabeth Terry came from pedigree. When a smart little WASP grows up around gardeners, third-world aristocrats, Eurotrash, and the most protected people on the planet, ultimately the other members of the inflated class are the only ones who can really see when something has gone very, very wrong. And that is the one thing that WASPs never want to discover. Because so much is already wrong: the privilege, the arrogance, and the superiority. So, when regular people look at it, they see the emblematic injustice. But, the depth of an individual's pathology? Indistinguishable.

Coming to work at her job as a New York City police detective after doing drugs at lunch was wrong. Maggie knew that for real, now. She didn't know that when she was doing it, because she was deluded. There is an overlap between addiction and arrogance. Why else does someone stick a needle in their arm for the first time? They know what's going to happen. They know people get addicted and their lives become hell, but they do it anyway. If she had slid into the station house on three martinis or Bloody Marys at breakfast, the guys would have attributed it to her religion: WASP Nonexistent. But doing proletarian drugs with blond hair and blue eyes was beyond any socially recognized transgression or overstep. It was too stupid to be understood.

"Michael." Lucy coasted the room, intelligently, seductively, appropriately insinuating and reasonable. She played her layers, that one.

"Lucy." He glowed.

"Michael, you have been so wonderful to me over these many years. All those wills and contracts and divorces." She smiled, so the staff laughed. Even Enid. "Sometimes it has been awful, really, and you've been so terrific."

Enid nodded. "Divorce is awful." She was commiserating with a celebrity but would have embraced anyone subjected to a divorce. "I have tickets to see your play."

"Lucy is on Broadway at the moment," Michael explained to Craig, Sandy, and Maggie, who he assumed never went to Broadway.

In Maggie's case, he was absolutely correct. But Craig had a family, he had in-laws, he had out-of-town guests from various universities and his fraternity, and Maggie guessed he would rather drop money on theater tickets than have to sit across the table and maintain a conversation. As for Sandy, well she was silent and therefore she must know something. She must know how little it would help her to tell Lucy Horne about all of her performances she had enjoyed and benefitted from, because it would only deposit her into the category of sycophant.

"Have you seen today's news?" Lucy asked, a haunted quality now.

"You mean Nelson Ashford?" Craig barely inflected.

"What about him?" Maggie blurted out.

"The Klan-loving head of the Department of Justice is dismissing all charges against his killer."

Maggie froze. Eddie was free.

"I'm sorry Craig, but that is not what Lucy is referring to." Mike was annoyed. Hillary was a fine topic for office politics but nothing too racial.

Whoa! Eddie Figueroa was going to walk. Oh my God, Maggie winced. She looked at Craig, but, having been reprimanded, he was now blank.

"More settlements on the West Bank?"

That had come from Sandy, now revealed to be the biggest freak of all, the most extreme, and also the most deceptive.

"No." Lucy glided, as smooth as lube for ladies. "I'm afraid there was a murder."

"Actress!" Maggie shouted. And there it was, lodged in her memory box, Nick Stammas behind the deli counter that very morning, holding up the *New York Post* and plopping it down next to her apple and tea. Finally, a new experience produced. One not demanding to be suppressed. A day in which nothing terrible had happened yet, except that Nelson Ashford was dead for no reason and Officer Eddie Figueroa was free without having to produce an explanation, but his family would be so relieved. Julio's wife. She would be so . . . justified. The headline: "Actress Strangled."

"Yes." Lucy looked her straight in the eye. Another blue-eyed blond, just like Maggie. Blue-eyed blonds threw silent recognition at each other constantly.

About how recessive they are, and therefore how untouched. "May I have some coffee?"

Sandy jumped up because this was her lapsed responsibility.

"Me too," Craig said, annoyed, taking advantage of the moment to get his needs met. Why does he always have to wait for someone else to ask Sandy to get them coffee before she would get him his?

Sandy left the room to serve and Lucy showed her hand, like an adult waiting for the child to go to bed before telling the story of a rape.

"That poor girl, in the newspaper. That sweet, sweet girl was in my play. That girl. My play. I want you to find her killer."

Murder. In a constant avalanche of unbearable memories and associations—Alina, Frances, Julio, crack, dope, Courvoisier and Coke, and coke—only *murder*, was useful to recall. Maggie knew a great deal about death. It had been her profession. Disemboweled, decomposed, decapitated bodies in elevators, on toilets, in washing machines, in swimming pools, garbage bags, subway tracks, in the arms of their killers, lovers, mothers, all of whom were guilty. Like Julio always said, "Once you've fucked someone, it's easier to kill them." The wall is down. The penetration is so natural. It's easier to break a neck that you've licked, sucked, and ravished. Overkill is the greatest sign of love. Why say, "I'm too anxious to negotiate the relationship right now," when you can end someone's life? Right? Pulverize rather than communicate. Murder is for people who cannot slow down. Every detective knows that. So, look for the person whose mind is racing.

"Lucy, have you met the latest member of our team?" That was Mike, his hand warmly on Maggie's back, trying to save her yet again. Poor guy. "Maggie Terry. She is our new in-house private detective. Maggie was my student at Columbia when she did her graduate work in criminology. One of my best teaching assistants. Eleven years at the NYPD and a loyal friend to my family. Now here with us on a permanent basis."

Enid squirmed.

"Nice to meet you." Lucy smiled, waiting for Maggie to take the lead.

"What was the victim's name?" Maggie picked up a pen from a pile in the middle of the table and pulled over a yellow legal pad, laid out so carefully by Sandy in preparation for such an impulse.

"Jamie Wagner."

Sandy came back in with coffee, serving Lucy from the right, cup handle pointed out. Sandy once worked in a restaurant, Maggie noted. A good restaurant. And then added: Maybe she still does.

"Do you . . . I'm sorry . . ." Lucy was so kind.

"I'm sorry, my name is Sandy."

"Sandy." Warm smile. "Sandy, do you have soy milk?"

"No, I'm so sorry."

"Almond milk? Cashew? Coconut?"

"We have two percent."

"I'll have two percent." Huge smile. "Thank you, *Sandy*. Thank you so very much."

Okay, Maggie was on instinct. Now for the order of events.

CHAPTER SIX

What do you do when your child is gone?

Maggie had been worried about bonding at first. She and Frances hadn't been together that long— okay, a few years—but it's never enough, sometimes. Then Frances hit thirty-five and decided that she was just going to do this thing. They were already living together.

"Better you than me," Maggie had said.

Later she realized that Frances had had the kid because Maggie was already so far down the rabbit hole; it was a kind of alternative. A way to assert her separateness, to put down the gauntlet so that Maggie would somehow magically get better. Or it was hostility or obliviousness. Or a solo escape plan. But the thing that bothered Maggie most of all was that Frances wasn't aware of any of this. She thought she *just wanted to have a baby.* Some people don't believe in the unconscious. The real truth was that Maggie didn't want Frances to have a child because she was afraid of change. But that was a secret, so she half-heartedly went along with it, and parenting doesn't work that way. And then, Maggie showed up late and blasted at the hospital and missed the actual birth, having to stare down Frances's family, who *could not believe* she was drunk again. And then, Maggie looked at the little thing, Alina, fighting for some kind of place in the world already, and she . . . *identified*. It hit her what an opportunity this was, to help someone get started and to be there for them. To maybe do one thing right. And that little girl, her eyes wide open, big and brown, her fists pumping, determined. Maggie fell in love right then, and she wanted her. And—this is the sick part—she thought that maybe this little person would actually love her, unconditionally, and she, Maggie Terry, could finally learn what that was like. She didn't realize it was supposed to be the other way around. How was she supposed to know that? She had never had a good parent. And neither did Frances, even though hers were at least present.

What was a good parent? All around her, folks in the same boat had made the wrong choice. There was an arrogance in their assessments. She heard it over and over again at NA and AA. Their parents had given them nothing they needed, so they would give their child everything they never had. Which was, unfortunately, too big to give. Detectives take care of other people, that's their social role. They come in when things have gotten out of hand and they try to reinstate a sense of order. They ask questions, and try to make people accountable. Society needs that. To get there she had to study and cohere and develop skills and be brave. She had to witness unbearable messes and pain. And she had to be systematic. She just couldn't do this for herself. But Maggie didn't want that moment, twenty years hence, when it was her own kid who became the parasite and couldn't take care of herself or anyone else. She didn't want to be responsible for producing another manipulator. That was one of her fears.

Frances did not try to convince her. It was happening. It didn't matter how Maggie felt. Frances was a nice person with a work ethic. She didn't come from the rotting privileged class. In her world, women had children. And that was that. She had siblings and they all had kids. She and Maggie just had to socialize on holidays with Frances's side of the family, and pretend that Maggie's side didn't exist. Sounded like a great plan, but they forgot one detail. Maggie was from *her* side of the family, and even if she never spoke to any of them again, that would never change.

And Frances used all of that against her in court.

"Did you tell your partner that you did not want to be a mother?"

"Yes," she said, having just barely crawled out of detox, unable to feel the floor or recognize her own shoes.

"Did you say, 'Better you than me'?"

"Yes."

"No more questions."

But the real stuff was just starting to become clear now. No one had ever tried to understand the reasons. That was something Maggie struggled with in

Program, not blaming other people for not asking her, not guiding her through the key questions of self-understanding. Most people have ambivalence about their children but very few admit it. Telling Frances the truth was a reach for intimacy, sharing. She didn't think it would end up in court. Frances had said okay, and then they let it go. So many times they had skated the surface of everything that mattered, and Frances let her do it. But that was blaming her for Maggie's own character defects, and she wasn't supposed to do that. She was supposed to be *understanding*, as her caring sponsor Rachel G. would explain, substituting the word *understand* for the word *blame*.

"Understanding why things happen is the opposite of blame," Rachel said on the phone, in person, and over coffee, three decades sober and sponsor to the world's worst cases. "People make mistakes and take wrong turns. Being mortal is about being vulnerable."

But Maggie knew that no one outside of a meeting felt that way. Everyone else walked down the street thinking of themselves as pure and clean. They had it together because they were better, and the job of people who are better is to point out the ones who are worse and punish them. All of society seemed to be organized like that. Whoever could, would punish. It was linked to opportunity. Like the judge who took away her child, who ruled no visitation. He was fine with treating her so badly, then when he went home, no matter how much pain he had caused, he was better than someone. He was better than her.

After her mother's self-destruction, the new wife Julie came along with a permanent martini in her left hand. Maggie might have been eight, she might have been lost, she might have been thinking about all the ways she wanted to die, the ways that other girls did not. She might have been alone and living with so much pain, too much for her small body. But there was one thing in her already-ruined short life that actually made sense, and that was drinking leftover cocktails as a way to fall asleep. First mother, then self, then Frances, then Alina, then alcohol, Xanax, heroin, cocaine, crack, Klonopin, and grass. That's a lot of absence. Also career, income, status, the trust of others, and her dear Julio. His patient presence, side by side in that car, the station house, the deli, the park. That was her catalog of loss. And now it was all her fault. When the person who does you wrong is you, really, what else is left to go?

Sandy returned to the conference room with two-percent milk.

"Thank you, *Sandy*." Lucy smiled and softened her eyes like it was a huge favor, one which can never be repaid.

Having fulfilled her mission, Sandy was now trustworthy enough that Lucy Horne continued to talk openly in front of her. She was a good servant, after all, loyal, meaningless, amnesiac, and invisible.

"I told the police officer nothing, of course," Lucy assured the room. She knew her way around the corner and would never be a liability. After all, Lucy had handled things the people in that room could never imagine and had no way to consider.

"I see." Michael made notes.

"I didn't lie."

"Of course." He made more notes.

"I am about to do a Disney musical. You know what they're like." She whispered now, not to be overheard by the gods, the kings, the people who had the power to make her afraid. "*They* won't tolerate any scandals." She was trembling. "I'm older now. If I want to keep working at a level that is . . . appropriate, if I want to have a meaningful life, I have to be very, very clean. No whispers. No outrages. And *no scandals*." There was a silence around the table, and everyone realized that for the first time that afternoon, Lucy Horne was actually being genuine. "It could all be all over. Like that." *Snap!* And then, she regained her dignity. "It is raining outside, but it cannot rain inside. You understand."

"McMaster!"

That was Sandy, still blotting up the coffee she had sloshed over Enid's cup.

"Absolutely." Lucy beamed. But she was irritated. "John McMaster. I did his *Tulips in the Summer Months* at the Taper, in LA."

"I love his work," Sandy said. And then she had the misfortune to recite. "It is raining outside, but it cannot rain inside, Father. You understand, don't you?"

Okay, so Sandy reads plays, Maggie noted. She surely can't afford to go see them. But even more interesting was what the receptionist had revealed about Lucy. She used lines from plays as part of everyday banter. In other words, there was always a script.

Sandy blushed and exited the room to resume her role as someone nobody wanted to notice.

Michael backed up his wheelchair and repositioned it at the table, in the manner of an able-bodied man crossing his legs to indicate a shift, or the necessity of one, in attention. "Lucy, we are your legal team. Everyone here is under confidentiality, and this conversation is entirely protected."

"I understand."

"Lucy." He was kind now. His strength, *now*. Understanding, given everything. "Do you know anything about this young girl's murder?"

Lucy smiled to herself on purpose. This meant that she would either dismiss the implication as absurd, or . . . "I know who did it."

Just then Sandy reentered with a fresh napkin for Enid and a plate of cookies that only Craig would eat. She placed a cup next to Maggie's yellow pad and whispered in Maggie's ear, "I brought you a mint tea."

How did she know? Maggie scanned her own range of misbehaviors over the day and landed right on her moment of entry when she had placed her takeout deli cup, already half on her blouse, on Sandy's desk and rudely left it there in the hubbub of ambivalent welcome. Sandy had had to throw it in the wastebasket, to clean up after her. On her *first day*. Was this mint tea an act of intimidation or care?

"Who?" Michael's voice was soft. He had bedside manner. "Who is the killer?"

"That young girl confided in me." Lucy shuddered and looked to the window, where, in an off-Broadway play, there would have been a crack of lightning, and at Lincoln Center, a full downpour. She wrapped her arms around her torso in a way that accentuated her breasts and then released them in an act of resignation. "She was being stalked."

Stalked. That word again. Maggie wrote it on her pad in quotation marks. It was one of those words that made everyone stop and defer, defying normal questioning, which then became its own act of aggression. It was a game changer.

"That was the word she used. Stalked."

"By who?" Michael knew his lines.

"A fan?" Enid asked.

"A *fan*? Jamie Wagner had not accrued any fans, poor thing. She played the serving girl. Brought in the coffee. Brought it out."

Maggie felt that somehow Sandy was being implicated. She looked around the table, but no one else seemed to notice.

"No," Lucy answered plainly. "It was an ex-boyfriend."

Everyone nodded. This was universally understood: ex-boyfriends stalk. Police officers, Irish lawyers, disabled shooting victims, divorcées, black IT geniuses, serving girls, actresses, receptionists, and drug addicts all accepted this reality of modern life. It was a fact in the same way that mothers' boyfriends molest, handymen expose themselves in school basements, priests are predators. Anyone who watched TV knew these incontrovertible facts. Ex-boyfriends always had a lot of explaining to do.

"The most important thing—" Lucy faltered, realizing that what she was about to ask for was in fact *not* the most important thing. "What I mean is . . . can you keep me out of this? Can you find the killer and make this all go away?"

"Of course." That was Michael, promising whatever needed to be promised.

"I hope we can bring this to a close before Disney and I start rehearsal."

"What's the show?" Michael, always on cue.

"*Buffalo Bill's Wild West.* I play the Indian queen who starts out as a curiosity but ends up winning Bill's heart, and in this way civilizes him. A more progressive reversal on the old cliché that asks who *really* is the primitive."

Maggie noticed Craig googling with such intensity that he should have been gasping for breath. Was he the kind of black man to say something about a white matron playing an Indian woman? She guessed not. Not after the reprimand from Mike for objecting to killer-cop Eddie Figueroa getting off scot-free. Maybe at home with his family he would riff on the ofays and their blond-haired Native American princesses, but Maggie would put money on his silence here.

She looked at him.

He stared at his device.

"Lucy," Enid asked, prepared to wrap this all up by the beginning of the first read through of *Buffalo Bill*, and anything else the famous actress and her corporate megapolis would want. "Do you know his name?"

"Steven Brinkley."

Craig searched.

"That sounds familiar." Enid scratched it out on her pad.

"Got it!" Now Craig could channel all his exasperation and put-uponedness into something acceptable *and* that got the job done. "National Book Award–winning author of *The Mere Future.*"

Triumphant, he held out his coffee cup for Sandy

to refill. She jumped up and reached for the pot, but it was empty. Another failure. She scrambled out to make more while Craig turned his cup over in its saucer.

"My memory isn't what it used to be. I just read that with my book club." Enid, ever the participant, reached into her purse, pulled out her Kindle, and waved it around, shaking her head at her own disappearing mind.

Maggie, always alert to potential tools of deception, noted that one could claim anything about a Kindle. It was like the cooking shows permanently playing on the community television in rehab. The only program she could actually stand was *Chopped*, a competition featuring real people, many of whom were fat or gay or brown or immigrants or some combination thereof, the kinds of people who fill the world but are only seen on television if they were accused of crimes or leading nations. They had to cook meals for "celebrity" chef judges she had never heard of out of absurd ingredient combinations like bubble gum, pig intestines, eggplant, and fish sauce. The judges would taste gingerly, and then declare how briny, soggy, light, or undercooked the concoctions were, and praise the cooks for heat, texture, and blended flavor that spectators could never experience. Maggie always thought the judges were lying. They didn't really eat that slop. There was no way for viewers to know what was truly on that plate, and how it actually tasted. They had to trust. Same with Enid's Kindle. It could have contained bondage porn or be broken, and the observer would never know. Perhaps she'd purchased it with the best of intentions but couldn't actually figure out how it worked, and carried around the empty thing looking to snag a brawny husband number three with her need for assistance; perhaps it was her mantrap.

"A full search of Jamie Wagner," Craig reported, "reveals that aside from her murder, and an appearance on *Law and Order*, there is almost nothing of note. She was in a production of George Bernard Shaw's *Arms and the Man* at the Berkshire Theatre Festival. That's about it."

"So what does that tell us?" Mike finally drank his now cold coffee.

"Well, what I want to know," Craig teased, genuinely smiling for the first time, thereby revealing that he was only happy when he knew something no one else had ever considered. "Why would a famous, successful man be dating an unknown actress? Steven Brinkley has five hundred thousand hits."

"Ah, men." Enid sighed.

Ignoring her undermining of his moment of glory, Craig showed his phone to the room. They passed around a photograph of a fairly average intellectual, white someone who did something right and was treated fairly. Brinkley looked healthy in a way that could translate to "good-looking" but might only have reflected that he was rested, had had a few facials in his lifetime, was an appropriate weight, and had gotten some sun.

"That is the killer," Lucy said, a bit less than aghast.

"Did you meet him?" Mike asked. "When he picked Jamie up from the theater?"

"I wouldn't know. A minor player's boyfriend is not someone who I would spend time with, it doesn't work that way. After the show I am swarmed with fans asking for autographs and then a car takes me home."

"Okay, then." Mike looked at his watch. He had a personal training session coming up at Equinox. "Craig, it's your case."

Craig beamed.

"Lucy, I will of course supervise his every move."

"What?" Craig could not believe this was happening to him, again.

"Maggie will be your assist."

"Oh, come on!" Craig protested, but then immediately recovered. He already knew that Mike never changed his mind until he had to. Remembering that there was a client present he produced a fake smile. "Okay."

"Great." Michael shifted his chair to indicate the end of the meeting.

"Lucy," Enid rose, "I'll see you to your car."

Lucy stood, performing gratitude, confidence, and relief that once again someone else would take care of what had to be handled so that she could take care of herself.

"Thank you all. And you, *dear*."

"Yes?" Maggie answered, reviewing her notes.

"Call my assistant and he'll send you some tickets."

"To what?"

"My show."

"What show?"

The rest of the team froze in horror, midair, at various stages of rising and reaching. No one filled the silence of Maggie's destroyed opportunity, so Enid and Lucy left the workers behind to take care of details.

"Sandy," Mike yelled, grabbing his gym bag. "Run downstairs and get Maggie a copy of *The Mere Future*."

"Okay, is there a bookstore nearby?"

"There must be, it's New York City."

Craig started googling. "The Strand. Twelfth and Broadway."

"Thank you." Mike didn't want to be bothered with too many details. "Take two cabs, we don't have time for Uber." And he was out the door.

Craig's mental gymnastics about how to sideline Maggie were legible in the furrow of his brow. He turned to her, grinned in a blatant display of pure annoyance, and said in the kindest *you know I'm kidding*, broadest buddy-buddy tone available on the human continuum of veiled threat, "Maggie." He showed his teeth. "I will watch you like a hawk."

Early evening in Manhattan. Summer. New Yorkers are soft and kind because they live in front of each other and understand the fragility of human complexity. New Yorkers are tough and crusty because they spend half the year sweating in a hotbox of bodies, surrounded by vermin and stinking garbage, and the other half freezing, in boxes without enough heat and rattling windows, waiting for the snowplows to get there. There was that one week, euphemistically known as "spring" when any stranger could naively think: What a delightful place to live. The cherry blossoms fill the trees, the sky is clear and bright, smiles and skin awaken each other. Everyone is sexy, people fall in love, and have great ideas that other people agree to allow to succeed. There is life. It is a remarkable moment of *yes, yes, yes.* And there is an excitement about living and forgiving and creating new worlds in the midst of this temporary beauty, this illusory restorative clarity, and this rare clean feeling. And then, suddenly, it is hot again. And everything droops: hopes, collars, and wills.

This summer, Manhattan Cable was tearing up the street because all the landlines in the neighborhood were completely down. The 4 train didn't run on weekends and the B train was on the D track and the L was going to be shut down for a year and a half. The governor had suggested that people in Williamsburg "use cars" to get to Manhattan, which wasn't going to happen. What cars? The most frequent existential questions overheard while waiting for the light to change were: Would the Orange One be impeached? Would he bomb a country run by someone as crazy as himself and begin the end of the world? Yes, the disordered were entirely in charge, it was the Borderline Apocalypse, people who couldn't nuance were making impulsive decisions about everyone else's fate.

Maggie knew that she should be sitting in an NA meeting, listening to someone else's pain, their process, obstructions, and desires. But instead she was hurriedly following Craig Williams, as he remained a half step ahead of her all the way down Eighth Street. One of the promises she had made to herself, and to her sponsor, Rachel, was to make 12 Step meetings as integrated a part of her life as eating breakfast. But both were turning out to be difficult to pull off. She hadn't expected to be working past six on the first day, but Craig acted like fieldwork was an expected part of the terrain, so she kept this rising anxiety to herself. The staggering quickly took on an observational tone as Maggie became aware of having to watch where she was going, *literally*, as so much had changed. Greenwich Village was Deadwood. Empty storefront after empty storefront. Where had it all gone? The shoe stores that had once lined both sides of the block were either black spaces or awkward restaurants that would never make it. Why was there a Domino's Pizza on Eighth Street? Why would anyone in Manhattan need a place to get bad pizza? The oldest head shop in New York was out of business, empty.

Eighth Street and Sixth Avenue had long been a favorite hangout for junkies. Ghosts hung around the shadow of the old Nedick's, where dopeheads lived for the mythological hot dog and orangeade next to beat-poet junkies, who were replaced by Warholian junkies, and then the subsequent junkies with no other purpose or cause besides junk. Now it was a former Barnes & Noble, the McDonald's of bookstores—carnivores, those two: Mr. Barnes and Mr. Ignoble. They had driven out so many independent businesses only to be themselves done in by Amazon, who had just purchased Whole Foods, destroying any illusion of wholeness, replacing it with homogeneity. Across the street was the empty Gray's Papaya with some letters pulled off of the marquee, and a sign proclaiming it would be replaced by a cold-pressed juice emporium. Every cop in New York City made it to Gray's Papaya for the "recession special": two hot dogs with mustard, sauerkraut, and grilled onions, and a powdered papaya drink for five bucks. No cops would buy cold-pressed juice. They didn't know what it was and couldn't afford to find out. No beacon from the storm left on the whole street, no place to find someone to talk to, to score from, arrest, or fuck. Just gone.

Craig stopped dead. Tapped his toe, waiting for her to catch up. "What's the matter?"

Maggie wasn't sure if he was actually asking her this question or was being rhetorical or critically encouraging her to walk faster.

"I really should be at a Narcotics Anonymous meeting right now."

"Holy shit," he said, first to himself and then to her. "Do not fuck up on my dime."

"Okay."

Then he looked at her sincerely, and yet practically. "Our appointment with Brinkley is at seven thirty. Where is the nearest meeting?"

She checked Rachel's now crumpled list. "Saint Veronica's Church on Christopher Street. At six thirty."

The clock on the Jefferson Court Library tower read quarter to seven.

"Okay, I'll give you thirty minutes."

While Craig waited outside, biding time amid the empty storefronts of Bleecker Street, Maggie did what people in Program call the Next Best Thing. She slid in late to a meeting that she should have been to on time, and took a seat in a folding chair laid out by someone else doing the service that she, herself, should have done.

Like most of the places that hosted meetings, Saint Veronica's was old fashioned, uncool, and a bit decrepit. Sitting in this wobbly folding chair produced the anxiety that Maggie had been repressing all afternoon. Her first day working sober. She realized she couldn't breathe. It felt like she had a blood clot in her lungs; it felt like there were ten. But really, it was just emotional. Normally she could take a Xanax or five, or four Klonopin and a shot, and later some dope and then another drink. Now, she had nothing except this meeting. The drugs took everything away and then they took the drugs away. Blah, blah, blah.

Someone was in the process of saying something that could either save her life or make her want to get high. It was a crapshoot, being conscious. Damper or trigger. Kind of like real life. Basements filled with mediocre thinkers, childish narcissists, and whiners, and then suddenly someone might get called on who could put together five words that would reach her heart and save what remained to keep it beating. She looked around. Faces were starting to feel familiar. But there were always new faces, too. Tonight, for the first time, she saw this masculine young guy, cute, with his hands wrapped around the thigh of a dynamically feminine young woman. They could have been models.

"My wife," he was saying. "My wife."

Clearly they were hanging on to each other for dear life. She was following him around the world to keep him from picking up and . . . maybe it would work, to be loved that much. Perhaps. They say you can't control other people, but plenty of people were controlling Maggie. What if the person you loved stuck by you, no matter what? The truth was, she suddenly understood, Maggie would never have left Frances. No matter how much Frances complained, no matter how much blame she laid, Maggie loved her and Maggie was loyal. She loved Alina with all her heart and she was loyal to her as well. She would never abandon them, ever. In the sense of "walking away." Being emotionally distracted was what *family* meant. But Maggie would never actually leave. She had to get them back. The fact was that if the tables were turned, and they easily could have been, Maggie would be there sitting next to Frances with her arm around her shoulders while her darling bawled out all the pain of her life. She would have helped.

"What's the matter with you? Are you drinking?" Frances asked the very first time she was supposed to be clean. Maggie could still see the surprise and hurt in her lover's eyes. Frances had not expected *it* to ever happen again. She actually thought stopping was that easy. Some counseling and a few meetings later and she thought they could get their lives back. "Oh my God, Maggie! Are you drinking?" It was still a real question. And Maggie had to say something. Frances was still waiting back then, waiting for her to promise that it wasn't true.

"Calm down, Frances. I had a glass of wine." Then she laughed. "And a bottle of wine." Then she really laughed. It was cruel, but it was also so, so sad. It was a joke, after all, the idea that things could be okay. That she wouldn't be the source of all the trouble. *The problem.* The problem wasn't the problem unless everyone else decided that it was. But when she stood in court and watched Frances take her baby away . . . Frances had done drugs too, of course. She'd also done coke, whatever. But Frances could take it or leave it, and Maggie would take it and leave. Did that make Maggie bad and Frances good? It was genes or something, something beyond the self. Maggie knew she deserved to be punished, but this was overkill. What happens when you're guilty too but are the only one punished? There was no way to appeal it. Overpunishment isn't one of those things that people know what to do with. You're supposed to suffer if you take drugs when you're not supposed to, and Maggie did and then calamity struck. And now this: calamity by the gallon, by the hour.

"My wife, my wife," the good-looking drug addict rambled. "Thank you." And then, narcissist that he was, he forgot to call on the next speaker until his wife whispered in his ear. He picked from the raised hands before him, desperate to be heard. And she felt so good about that. The wife. That she had helped. She was on his side, no matter what.

It was just like Julio, who couldn't stand the idea that his son was a bully cop. He couldn't believe it. The newspapers had *his kid*, Eddie, taking out Nelson Ashford, a black man in the Bronx, for reaching for his keys. It was all over the news; there were witnesses and there was a rumor of cell phone footage.

"Fuck those cell phones," Julio said. "Anyone can shoot something with a cell phone and pretend it's real."

It just broke his heart, to see his son maligned like that. To see his name on the cover of the *Daily News*.

OFFICER CHARGED WITH MURDER

To see the posters carried by Black Lives Matter.

STOP POLICE VIOLENCE.
JUSTICE FOR NELSON ASHFORD.

It crumpled Julio. He couldn't stand it.

"We have to be there for each other," he said, meaning family but also meaning blue brothers, the NYPD. "If there is no respect for the police, then there is chaos."

Sitting in the unmarked car that detectives always drove, Maggie watched Julio's torment. Months passed, days after days of Eddie being placed on leave, and still the Ashford family wanting to press charges. She watched Julio cry, she saw him weep.

"Let's all rise for the Serenity Prayer."

That again. It always came to that. Standing up and holding hands. Then everyone would start in unison with the word *God*. But Maggie never said this. She didn't believe in God, and she didn't want to start anything that was supposed to be sincere with the word *God*. So, she would be silent as everyone else shared the first word. After that she would join in.

Was that her mistake? Not saying *God*? Was that going to be the ultimate downfall of her Program, a sign of her lack of admission to helplessness? She knew she was helpless, but not to God. She was helpless to Frances and Alina and judges and people who felt they were better than her. But those people existed, for the moment, and God did not. How was she going to get better if she couldn't get through the third step? "Made a decision to turn our will and our lives over to the care of God as we understood Him." But she did not understand. And there was no Him.

Suddenly, she was out on the street.

"What are you doing out so fast?" Craig was cramming what must have been a second slice of pizza into his face. She could tell because he was no longer savoring it, just eating it. He looked at his Apple watch. "You still have three minutes." He had been counting on them to digest.

"I couldn't go there today."

"Go where?"

"The wreck."

"Whatever." He lost interest.

Nice guy, Maggie realized. And she felt blessed that in his crotchety way he was trying to support her. And then she felt nauseous; it was all sooooo upsetting.

"Okay then." He wiped his mouth. "Let's go pay a visit to . . ."

". . . the *Stalker*."

And they both sang the theme of cartoon villains everywhere: *Dum, duh, dum, dummm . . .*

This momentary camaraderie earned by Craig's compassion soon withered after twenty minutes of futilely waiting for Steven Brinkley to show up on the steps of his Perry Street townhouse, down the block from the one used on *Sex and the City*. Craig kept looking at his phone as Maggie watched legions of young women posing for selfies in front of the house before going off for their collective bonding over cosmos. She wanted one. She wanted two. She wanted that sickly Kool-Aid whiff when they were made badly, and the way a bump of coke fixed all of that. And the illusion of cleansing that came when a cocktail was made well, with fresh ginger and blood orange juice added to the poison, the delight, the fix. The first sip and then the moment it all kicked in. The relief.

"Where is that dickhead?" Craig was fed up. "Fucking famous people. He's a half hour late. My daughter needs . . ."

"What does she need?"

"She needs me to help her write a report."

Broken heart.

Wanting to show how appreciative . . . wanting to be able to thank . . . wishing for the authority the world had once handed her . . . missing Alina more than everything, of course she now had *homework*. How could Maggie be so selfish to not have realized that. Alina would soon start first grade. She had friends. She had crushes and fights. She had an entire reality in which Maggie was not a speck of dust.

"Go home, Craig." Maggie stepped up to a plate that she could not reach.

"Right. Not funny!"

"For real. Go home to your family. You can catch the end of dinnertime. Your kids are waiting. Brinkley may never show and you know it."

It was the *you know* that would let him say yes. Like they were both facing the fact that this meeting wasn't happening, so he could feel okay about letting her take the weight. That's what assistants are for, after all. Right?

"Okay."

She knew that meant *thanks*.

"I'll see you in the office tomorrow at nine." He was stern, like she needed a warning even though she hadn't done anything wrong. He looked at his phone. "Oh, shit."

"What is it?"

"The North Koreans tested a ballistic missile."

"Wait," she remembered. "I have an NA meeting at eight."

"Okay, I'll pick you up there at nine."

"Great, the Greek Orthodox church on Sixteenth Street between Sixth and Fifth."

"Look," he said, shouldering his bag. "Call me whenever . . . if anything happens."

"Will do." She felt better. Someone was letting her decide something.

"I mean *anything*. Even if you think something *might* be happening but you're not sure."

"Okay." There was a hot breeze on her neck. She could feel something.

"I want to know everything you know."

"Got it."

"And Maggie, if anything comes up on my end I'll text you. What's your cell?"

"I don't have one. The place came with a landline, but the cables are down. If you call, it goes to voicemail."

"How are you going to check your voicemail if you don't have a phone?"

She hadn't considered this. "A pay phone?"

Of course he didn't trust her, she didn't make any sense. "When was the last time you saw a pay phone?" Craig looked at her transparently. She was detrimental to his apparatus. She was a fucking mess.

"Fix it," he said with finality because he wanted to go home, not because he believed it was possible.

"Okay."

She watched him walk away and leaned back on Brinkley's elaborate stoop. She could run away and get drunk. She took out her copy of *The Mere Future* and started to attempt reading as Craig hurried off to the subway home.

The first few words of the novel didn't process. She tried again.

Before the young woman approached, he had already rejected her.

Maggie did not understand. Why reject other people? They might need you. But wait, maybe a surprise was in store. Maybe it was one of those unreliable narrators who would learn the most important lesson of all: that other people are real and need our mercy. She had not read an entire book in years, perhaps decades. Paperwork, yes. But a novel from beginning to end? Not unless it was *The Big Book*, or *Courage to Change*, or *How Al-Anon Works*. She didn't have space. Maggie tried again.

Her wounds glowed like desire.

Why reject somebody because they are wounded? That was the whole problem, wasn't it? She regretted not having stayed the three extra minutes at the NA meeting. Where else were illusions of one's own perfection so quickly dispelled?

They illuminated all the lives she had ruined before she'd noticed his, from across the room.

She closed the cover, looked at the author photo on the rear jacket. Tanned, on a sailing skiff, laughing.

Probably an asshole. Being a detective always re-minded her that some people are a surprise, but not everyone. That was the problem, after all, jumping to conclusions without evidence did not pan out 25 per-cent of the time. If she had to make a snap decision because a house was on fire, it was right to assume that the big, muscled fireman could carry her and the tiny, skinny guy could not. But then later she might find out that the muscle queen OD'd on steroids and his arms were imploding, just for show. The little guy, however, was a tai-chi master and could decapitate bad people with his pinkie finger. Still, rich men who advertise their boats and came late to meetings with investigators working on the murder of their girlfriend were probably not the nicest, most caring lot.

"Hey," someone called out. "Are you Maggie Terry?"

Is it my dealer? was her first thought. Then she remembered that like a mother and a daughter and a lover, she no longer had a dealer. All she had was this moment, this book in her hand that she didn't want to read, this job she was not ready for, and the unlike-able man coming up the street. That was her real life. Today.

CHAPTER EIGHT

8:30 PM

Steven Brinkley ran up as though he had been running for a fortnight, leaping over streams, avoiding gunshots, evading police on horseback only to fulfill his promise to make it to Maggie's feet. This was supposed to assure her that, in spite of his gallant show of integrity, evil exterior forces had conspired to make Brinkley an hour late. He had an embedded *no fault of my own* air about him, carried by the impressive ability to run at his middle age without much sweat. Only one day back in the real world and Maggie had already learned—by comparing Craig to Mike—how to identify men with personal trainers who go to all their sessions, hit punching bags, train for marathons, and throw barbells with hired young men of color egging them on. Perfection was a fad, apparently, like the bitter, algae-rich, scum-encrusted lake water she imagined when she saw the words *cold pressed.* Or

Gyrotonics, which she had at first assumed was a new kind of Greek meat served from a spinning skewer with raw onions. She imagined all the announcements of *gluten free* to be a call for gluttonous Americans to just stop overeating.

"I'm sorry I kept you waiting."

He lightly hopped up the stairs, smiling, showing again his great shape and that he, at somewhere in his late forties, still had full control of his muscles as well as his neurons, hair follicles, hearing, skin tone, sight, lymph system, and sphincter.

Brinkley, ever the gentleman, indicated for her to precede him, and so she stepped forward, ladylike, and approached the imposing entranceway. His front door was a hand-carved dark wood. It had probably been on that house since the days of Edith Wharton. That it had remained intact and unmolested on this picturesque side street of wealth and comfort was miraculous, so she already knew there was a security camera poised in the thick trees shading the sidewalk. Maggie ran her hand over the door's sculpted vines, grapes, and leaves that bordered its imposing presence. Brinkley pulled his keys out of his tailored jacket pocket and pushed open the door, again holding it for her like the gentleman scribe he certainly intended to be.

"After you."

She entered. "Thank you."

"Miss Terry."

That was the gentleman's fishing expedition to find out if she was married and to let her know that he was trying to find out.

"Maggie."

"I want to do everything I can to help." Then the door closed behind them.

It wasn't this offer that threw her, most people in his position said something along those lines. Often they were almost sincere. But help *what*? Human relationships were complicated and that didn't mean they were corrupt. Did he want to help her find the killer? Yes, if it wasn't him. Did he want to help her see things his way? Perhaps that, too. Sometimes there was more at stake than life and death.

Technically this was an innocent man whose inappropriately paired, too-young girlfriend had just been murdered. How was he supposed to act? Some people are destroyed when a murder enters their life. They can't conduct normal business. They become permanently shocked, obsessed with justice, or feel overwhelmingly endangered in an act of recognition or projection. None of these applied in his case. If Steven Brinkley was in fact guilty of the deed himself, well, murderers who thought they could get away with it usually employed histrionics or the contrast, a deep cold. A quiet. But most murderers didn't *think*. They were overcome by need, controlled by it, and planned the cover-up with hindsight, when it was too late to hide. Steven Brinkley was a celebrity. His skills at sociality extended far beyond the average citizen. He engaged with fans, with colleagues, with media daily, and had done so for at least two decades. He knew how to show interest, how to appear to be available, and how to do the hard work of making other people feel at ease. Therefore, he had a natural public face designed for others' consumption. And the fact that he could wear it as well as his antique watch and hand-cut belt told Maggie nothing more than simply that.

They walked into his den, instantly comforting and familiar, like a seminar room in the old Vassar library. Which, in turn, was much like the private studies of some of the fathers of some of the girls who attended Vassar. Maggie was one of those girls. The den had books that created possibility, the chance that one could read them or write them or become the subject of them. After all, a writer worked here. He made *those* books and read *these* books; they were not for show. They were experiences, not objects. And, since it was comfortable and dynamic and clearly in use, if expensive, it was ultimately functional. This was a place to consume literature in order to produce it.

"Thanks for reading my book."

"I've only read two sentences."

"Thanks for telling the truth."

She looked up and, without thinking, started perusing the shelves. It was a wonderful library, the kind that invited immediate inspection, more of that tactile carved wood, beautiful editions in loving condition. She walked along, inhaling more than reading the spines. Hart Crane. Carson McCullers. Claudia Rankine. Rabih Alameddine. She opened a copy of Tennessee Williams's *Memoirs*. Signed, of course. *To Buffie Johnson with love, Tom.*

"Who is Buffie Johnson?"

"An obscure, great iconoclastic artist of the twentieth century. Passed away now. She had two husbands and two girlfriends and lived to be ninety-four. I met her at Yaddo when she was blind but still painting.

She was painting spheres. Her boyfriend was an old crotchety minimalist, Clayton something. She once had a relationship with Patricia Highsmith, apparently. One of her husbands died of AIDS."

He can do this forever, Maggie thought. Tell classy stories that are half gossip, half history.

"Excuse me." He smiled. "I'll be right back." Brinkley stood silently and gave her space, stepping out and disappearing somewhere into the house.

Could he tell that she was queer? Was that the reason for all the girlfriend/AIDS talk? Normally straight people didn't point out other people's girlfriends, but it's a different world now. They want to have everything. The stakes of cool masculinity were ever on the rise.

Left alone with classics of heart and taste, this room was a special breed of refuge, and, unlike most familiar things from Maggie's past, it was comforting. She appreciated that. She glided along a bit and saw herself in an antique mirror set quietly among his books. She allowed herself to stare, fully taking in how both plain and exhausted she looked. Finally, Maggie saw what everybody else saw. Someone who had squandered all her opportunities and talents and whose life was over. Or almost over. Or even worse, would go on and on in this state of waste. Her eyes welled with tears. How would she ever keep them back? She had to. Her heart attacked her composure. It was an internal struggle, heat and anxiety overcame her and she started to sweat. Maggie just stood still. There was no way out of any of it. This was who she was, and this was her life. She had spoiled it all.

She turned away from the mirror at the sound of Brinkley's footsteps coming purposefully down the hall. He carried a tray, silver of course, with evening tea and some delicately crafted cookies, purchased from someone who worked with their hands.

"It's a detective novel," he said, setting the tray down on the coffee table, actually used for coffee and perfectly reachable within the socially arranged configuration of embracing sofas and relaxing armchairs. So far everything in the house that was beautiful was functional, in applied use for human relations.

"What is?" She wiped her face with the back of her hand.

"My novel. The one you didn't read."

Wake up, she told herself. You are working. Get with it and stop wasting time. "Forgive me for asking, but do you usually write about detectives?"

"Not at all," he smiled, acknowledging that she was in fact a detective and yet behaving entirely unthreatened by the thought that Maggie may know more about being a detective than he did, and therefore he may have gotten some of it very, very wrong. He seemed nice, somehow, and he seemed happy to have someone to talk to. His lover had just been murdered, after all.

Maggie sank down into the soft leather sofa. It was perfect. She could have rolled up into a little ball and cried under a big comforter and then slept peacefully until someone bearing homemade soup swooped in with a feathery kiss—an event that was far, far out of reach. No kiss, no nap, no someone, no comforter, no comfort, no soup, but *today*, a person did bring her tea on a tray with little pretty cookies. That was something.

"My first book was a mystery, and I have come back to that now, so many years later, so much better a writer, so much more knowing." He poured the steaming ginger tea into a handmade mug, she guessed a sentimental gift from a friend. "You know the trope—one person, the detective, wants to understand. The other, the guilty party, doesn't want to be punished. But why the guilty one committed the transgression, and why it is in fact a transgression, and whether or not punishment is appropriate at all is ultimately up to the reader to uncover and decide. The detective has his own burdens and conflicts, and sometimes those of the illegal act he is charged with investigating match some of his own demons, and sometimes they match too well."

"What's the crime?" She sipped the tea, bright, probably organic, and freshly alive.

"A drug thing." Brinkley drank his tea. "And you know what that means, as an officer of the law. We all have addictions, but when illegality is involved, the person has extra problems."

She was, of course, no longer an officer of the law. "Like what?"

"Well, they have to hide, which means they have to lie. They have to be a great judge of character because they want something from everyone they meet. And they have to be willing to write some people off because when you are on a big full-time hustle, there are . . ."

"Losses?"

"Well, I was thinking more of the term *collateral damage*. It's unavoidable. Like Trump trying to roll back the EPA's methane restrictions and the courts,

God bless them, trying to stop him. But God, let's not get into that bottomless swamp."

"The courts matter." Maggie reached for a cookie. What would it be? Would she like it? "Is the book arguing for drug legalization?" She bit into it. Chewy, it stuck to her teeth. Maybe she didn't like cookies.

"Absolutely. Too many people are in jail and Trump . . . You seem upset."

Men and gay women had always been nice to Maggie. They were susceptible to her looks. They respected her beauty for the most fucked-up reasons. Frances came calling when she saw her baby blues. Julio was the only one who really loved her for her mind, when it was working.

"I'm sorry," she almost cried. "I'm having a rough day . . . month . . . year." She noticed the photographs framed on the paneled walls, autographed glossies of Marilyn Monroe, Vivien Leigh, Jean Harlow.

"So am I," he almost laughed. It was one of those unpretentious moments of honest acknowledgment that things could hardly be worse, and there was no reason and no way to pretend otherwise. "Maggie, you know what my problems are. Do you want to tell me what's troubling *you*? I'm a good listener. It happens to everyone."

That shocked her back into reality. Steven Brinkley had just revealed the fact that he was a shit. He had played it one step too far and exposed himself. He was a manipulator. And a user. She could see it all splayed out on the oak walls before her. If he was for real, there would only be one thing that concerned him: the death of his lover Jamie Wagner. Not getting laid by a stranger. Not grooming her by letting her self-indulge when she should be solving the case. This revealed him to be a user of the most sophisticated set. He allowed others to do things they had no right to do. This turned the attention on them, indebted them, made them complicit, and then gave him crucial information, letting him off the hook. He was dangerous.

She pointed to the photographs. "You have a soft spot for damaged beauties."

"I guess you could say Jamie fit that description."

He took it well, the deflection. Brinkley could play every angle, and knew instinctually to bring it back to the matter at hand, his own possible guilt. It was a typical ploy used to avoid accusations of setting up tangents. "She could have been a great actress someday."

"Why?"

"Because the only place she let herself really feel was onstage. There, she thought she knew how the story would end. With applause, not murder. She felt she had control. Life is, of course, unpredictable. So only onstage was she safe to live it. Actors have a repetition compulsion, you know. They do the same controlled thing in the same controlled, yet open, way. Over and over and over. And each time people, who in real life would shun and abandon and condemn, just sit back and applaud. Sometimes they even stand up." He raised an eyebrow in collusion. Mr. Brinkley was sussing Maggie out at the same time that she was reading him. It was a double-headed fuck. "That kind of release is what theater people call *emotional transparency*." He tapped his fingers on the table. He was thinking.

"What does that mean?"

"That they're only really alive when they act, and the explosion of feeling is infectious. Like someone locked up in the chains of their fragile emotional life suddenly bursting free onto a daisy-filled field. The world loves watching wounded beauties. I have some handmade caramels, a friend brought them over."

"No thanks."

"Once I understood how much pain Jamie was in, I accepted her exactly as she was. Every flaw. Every strange behavior." He recovered smoothly from her rejection of his candy.

"Well, that was nice of you."

"Well, it didn't work."

"Why not?" Maggie was exhausted.

He didn't react, but instead unwrapped a caramel and popped it in his mouth. She saw that he was annoyed she didn't eat one; he couldn't hide it.

"You know, Maggie, some people love you for what you can do for them. I am not that way. I love someone because that's how I feel. I can forgive anything and I would always take the person back."

"Unusual." *Familiar.*

"With Jamie, it became a dangerous kind of forgiveness. One that kept me from seeing that something was very, very wrong."

"What was wrong?"

"Well . . ." He hesitated like he was looking for the right words to express a concept he had been carrying, unarticulated, in his heart for a long, long time. But she knew that wasn't possible. He was a writer; he would stop the world's turn to find the right language. She could see that Steven Brinkley was lying. Again.

"Do you—"

"Every time." He cut her off. "Every time we reached a new level of intimacy, she would . . ." He paused again, assured she had learned her lesson and learned how to wait. Maggie understood now that he knew exactly what he was going to say. In fact, that he had said it before. And that this performance of hesitation was another trick to achieve a fake intimacy with her. "She would, I don't know . . . act out."

"Act out?"

There was something wrong with Jamie Wagner, emotionally. That's what Brinkley was trying to convey without coming out and saying it. He wanted to insinuate it, he wanted it to be understood. And he could be right. He was probably right. But what did that have to do with being strangled?

"Yes," he said, and sat back gravely so they could both ponder. Together. The poor dead girl who "acted out," and now look. Now look at what had happened.

The ginger was affecting her; Maggie's system was so clean that these things actually made a difference. And the sugar in the cookie hit her as well. She felt a bit light-headed.

Act out?

Act out.

Act out?

Steven went off to make some more tea, leaving Maggie enervated, tired, driven. A troubled, talented girl was dead. And it had something to do with acting out, a reality and an accusation she knew very intimately.

It had been an old neighborhood bar in Chelsea, opened by the original Georgie in the 1950s for his longshoremen buddies to stop off on their stumble home from the piers on West Street. Then, in the sixties there was a lot of construction, and much less shipping, so workingmen moved into building and that was a hard day's labor, deserving of a few cold beers. The city threw up those boxy projects and the sites were "union only," which meant white. The neighborhood's residents had always been mixed, even before the projects, mostly Puerto Ricans coming over in the thirties who weren't welcome a few blocks north in Hell's Kitchen, an ugly Irish ghetto. By the seventies, the gay boys discoed off the Greyhound buses by the thousands, and they loved Chelsea and they loved to drink. But each party in the neighborhood coexisted with the other, and people mostly stayed in their own spaces, recognizing that respect for territory was necessary to urban health.

By the time Frances and Maggie had found Georgie's, the old man was in a home and George Jr. was trying to bring things up to date. He got some modern beers, like Corona, plus Guinness on tap. He put in some shelf liquors like Stoli and Absolut. In those days, the gays started to order Ketel One and Grey Goose by the label, so he got those, too. The TV still blared, but George put in cable. That way, customers who used the bar as a home and other drinkers as a family could watch sports, the Oscars, and prestige series finales like *The Sopranos* or *Breaking Bad*. It was the mixed queer/straight place to go to after work for people who were comfortable in working-class environments and wanted to pay working-class prices. And those kinds of places always attracted people who liked to drink a lot and didn't really care about the decor. It was a place to be free from on-the-job rules, from the surveillance of coworkers, from one's self. *Home* for most people is quiet, with a kitchen, a TV, a bed with a warm body. But for an addict, those walls mean anxiety and reflections of one's own reverberating failures. Georgie's was where Maggie was safe . . . from what? From being exposed.

Things had been tough with Julio ever since Nelson Ashford reached into his pocket and Eddie thought it was for a gun. Or at least, that was what he claimed.

What was Eddie doing there in the first place? It was his precinct, but it wasn't exactly his beat. Maggie assumed something fishy was going on; it sure looked that way. Eddie was out trying to get something that no cop was ever supposed to be seen trying to get. And, for some reason, Nelson Ashford got in his way. It was late, and Ashford had worked a long day at UPS; he'd smoked a joint on the walk home from the subway. Both Maggie and Julio knew it would be used against his corpse in court. A person who is killed by a police officer cannot have ever done anything wrong. They cannot have failed a class in school, they cannot have kissed a girl who wasn't sure, and they certainly cannot ever be known to have taken drugs, especially on the night of the killing. That's what Julio had been talking about all day.

"The man was high; he could not have had good judgment. No one who's sober would ever threaten a police officer."

They were sitting in the radio car. Maggie knew she had to hurry because it was date night with Frances, but Julio was reviewing all the evidence.

"Did he threaten Eddie? Is that what Eddie's saying now?"

"Not verbally."

Julio was grasping, she knew it. He was in so much pain. His best son, the one who had grandfathered into the police department.

"Eddie never would have shot someone unless they were acting crazy. I know it."

Maybe it was because Julio had never smoked a blunt in his life, but Maggie knew the two events were not related. But she didn't say anything. Her pal was suffering, that's what mattered. Loyalty. But by the time they said goodnight she was agitated, both for Julio and for the tension of having something she could not honestly talk to him about. His son. So she was running late for what was supposed to be a romantic dinner between lovers. Whoever had thought up *date night* for long-term couples should have been shot on the spot. It was all about creating pressure and then shining a light on everyone's inadequacies. There was pressure to prove that one was loveable, pressure to keep up her end of the conversation, to show she was interested, to ask the right questions, to try to get the fucking discussion going in a way that would bring them closer. Not to fall into old traps of unresolved conflicts and problems that never went away, that was not the goal of *date night*. They were supposed to discover a delicious new dinner in a place that was affordable where people could hear each other think. Did that even still exist? And all through dinner they both knew they would have to fuck when they got home, or get off somehow, to show what was really in their hearts, something they both loved and had committed to and had forgotten how to name. Maggie picked up her super-sexy dress from the dry cleaner and put it on in the Georgie's bathroom. It was tight, white, a cut that made everyone imagine the Brazilian wax and pink nipples holding their secrets. She was supposed to meet Frances at the new Mexican place off Eighth Avenue and have fun over margaritas, but since she was at Georgie's changing, she did a line of coke with one of the forklift guys. If she was going to be charming, she would be fucking charming. And if she did another line, she would actually love being charming as opposed to hating it. Poor Julio.

After two drinks to take the edge off the coke, which was speedy, she faced the reality that she was going to be late, so she texted Frances to meet her at the bar. Maybe they could make out a little in the corner and get Frances to dinner with some excitement under her belt. Then those margaritas would be more fun. Like the seductive flirt Frances actually wanted, and the whore Frances really wanted to be. Frances was horny, and that took the pressure off. Maggie could see her shifting on the barstool. It was fun. This was Maggie's idea of fun. Turned on in public, making sure there was no private.

Maggie just couldn't bear to be anxious. Not that night. Not when Julio was so upset, and Eddie's case was certainly going to be an ordeal unless the commissioner could just bury it, but there were cell phones. Someone had a cell phone and too much footage for the white shirts to ignore. Anxious. Anxious. Maggie's shrink said she had anxiety because she had trouble "tolerating difference," but why the fuck would that be true? She was surrounded by it. There was no one like her within a mile of her life. He didn't know what he was talking about. "Things bother you that don't bother other people because of your father. When someone sees something differently from the way you do, you feel like you're going to be annihilated. But Maggie, with awareness, this can change."

After Frances decided to have fun, too, and downed her second Maker's Manhattan—this never came up in court of course, *her* drinking. Everything was on Maggie. With straight people, the mother gets away with murder, and with lesbians it's the birth mother who is presumed to be the hero. She did what she was supposed to do, after all, even if she is queer: she had a kid! After Frances's second drink she was turned on by Maggie's hand on her thigh and the ball game on the TV. She started cheering the Yankees, and then the news came on and it was all about the rumored cell phone footage that a neighbor claimed to have of Eddie Figueroa shooting Nelson Ashford, and it looked really, really bad for Julio. Eddie was coming off like a racist, like a maniac, like he didn't give a damn about a man's life.

"Damn. Remember that party, when he graduated?" Frances shook her head. "His parents were so proud."

"He's fucked."

"Come on, sweetheart." Frances patted Maggie's ass. "Let's go home and fool around."

"Come on, George. One more cosmo."

"I'm going out for a smoke," George said, too smart to get between Maggie and Frances. "Johnny will take over the bar."

"Come on, honey. We got to get going."

"I said *just one more*, Frances. Come on, Johnny, let's get some service over here."

Johnny was George's useless nephew, a friendly dickhead who had dropped out of Aviation High School and had some stupid tattoos, but the new kind. The kind that make no sense. Who wants a word on your neck and another on your knuckles? What kind of moron does that to his future?

Johnny raised his eyebrows to Frances, then made a big show of turning in Maggie's way. "I heard you the first four times."

"Frances is not in charge of me," Maggie snarled. "Are you, baby?" She licked Frances's face.

Now Frances was in a pout. They both sat there for a while watching the news, but Maggie was still feeling Frances's body, all over the place, and she was still turned on, even though she was mad. At this point George came back from his smoke and resumed control of the bar.

Maggie knew Frances was falling into some kind of a hole. Now the fun was over but she was still horny. She was already drunk but if she had another drink, it would be to keep quiet. Otherwise, everything would come pouring out. How wrong everything was. Not that Frances didn't want things to be better, she did. But Maggie could not give in, and Frances had decided that Maggie was her problem. She only knew how to shut down the conflict by escalating the drinking until the other person didn't care anymore about being in control. Like, if Frances said, "Maggie, I am fucking upset about the way we're living," then she already knew that Maggie would say, "Don't talk to me like that." And they would never be able to discuss.

"Welcome back, Georgie. Let me have my drink."

At that point Maggie must have been more sloshed than she realized, slurring or stumbling or something, because she could see in George's eyes what was happening. He was going to enter the conspiracy to cut her off.

"Okay, babe," Frances murmured in that way of

making everything worse by being condescending. Somewhere along the line she had internalized the false information that if she spoke softly and showed some love, Maggie would obey. But it was a rotten theory, because that soothing act enraged Maggie. How dare Frances love her when she was being forced to do something she didn't want to do. That's not love. Love is when you do what you want, even if you are in a relationship. Control was not love.

Maggie blew up. She knew she would. She always did. And Frances knew what was coming as soon as she started contradicting Maggie. So, why did she contradict her? What did she expect? It was damned if you didn't.

"Don't tell me what to do."

"Come on, Mags."

"Who the hell are you?"

Frances always got uptight at that point. When it wasn't fun anymore. "Come on, Maggie. We have stuff to drink at home."

"I don't want to go home."

That was it. She should be able to do what she wanted to do or else it was abuse. After all, Frances was trying to control her.

"We have a little girl at home with a babysitter who hates you as much as I do right now."

"You hate me?"

"I don't hate you, Maggie, and you know it. I just hate this shit." Frances pointed to her heart.

"If you hate being with me, you hate me."

"Maggie, I don't hate you. I just can't stand how you act."

"Same fucking thing." She knew she was being difficult but *fuck it*. Then Maggie crawled onto the bar, showing everyone her thong, as she meowed at the bartender. "Come on Johnny." She hissed and arched her back, made pretend scratch moves into the air.

"STOP ACTING OUT." That was Frances, at the end of her rope. But she was drunk, too. That was the thing that the court never heard a peep about. Frances also got loaded. "STOP ACTING OUT. When are you ever going to learn?"

CHAPTER TEN

10:15 PM

"Is everything okay?"

Maggie looked up. Steven Brinkley was concerned. He performed concern, his voice was soothing, his distance was perfect, his attention was present.

"I'm sorry, I was thinking."

"Happens to the best of us." He laughed and sat back in the chair. He was waiting to see if he had successfully beaten this thing, this round of investigation.

"So." Maggie reached for another cookie she didn't want. "She would act out. Jamie."

"Yes."

"I see." She had lost control of the moment by drifting away and that was lousy form. She had to get back the upper hand but fortunately Maggie knew how. She just waited. She didn't smile. She didn't move. She made the air heavy with the expectation that he would explain himself. Tell what he knew. About Jamie.

What she did. The dead girl. The one who acted out and got herself strangled by somebody else. Not by the man who knew something was wrong.

"One night we were sleeping together. At her place."

"Where did she live?"

"East Eighty-Second Street. Far eastside. In a boxy studio with no light and a fold-out couch and no air, over a woman who lived with her disturbed adult son. They used to bicker all the time. We could hear them yelling through the floorboards. It made everything even more unpleasant."

"Did Jamie ever come over here?"

"Sure. But we traded. I didn't want her moving in until she was more established financially. You understand. It wouldn't have helped anyone. Too much dependency."

Maggie nodded. Whoa, he was planning a future. That was a surprise. He was establishing boundaries. He believed she could make it. He thought that they could *do* it. That was reasonable. Adult. Maggie was thrown. She hadn't expected real plans, real love. She hadn't expected he would be so thoughtful. She didn't think he really cared, but now it seemed like he did.

"So." Brinkley sighed. Thinking. Feeling. His voice cracked. Paused. Then resumed. "So, we were sleeping. The doorbell rang. It was the middle of the night."

Maggie waited.

"The weird thing was that she hopped out of bed and just buzzed this person in. She didn't even ask who it was."

"And who was it?"

"Her father." Brinkley's tone was exhausted and

incredulous. Not a welcomed father, obviously. Maggie finally heard some pain. "The man entered her place like it was normal to barge in on his daughter at 3:00 a.m."

"Was he drunk?"

"No, worse." For the first time, Maggie thought that he would cry. "And she didn't even put on a bathrobe."

"She sat naked in front of her father?"

"No, no, no. But in a skimpy thing. And she didn't have a second thought about it."

"Was he embarrassed?"

"No, it was a conspiracy between the two of them. It was how they normally conducted their lives. All the imposition. He sat there, at the edge of our bed, mumbling incoherently—monologuing, really—about all kinds of insane subjects. Barely noticing that I was there in my skivvies with the blanket pulled up to my chest."

"What did they talk about?"

"Arcane philosophy. Bizarre and extremely inappropriate sexual theories. Tagore. He was rambling on and on about the Indian writer Tagore. And about Chekhov and sex. Big subjects but insubstantial commentary. The kinds of things a father doesn't say to his daughter, especially while she is in bed with a naked man. He's a truly sick person. Anyone would feel that way about him. It was obvious."

"Except Jamie."

He pointed at Maggie. "You are correct."

This was a whole new turn. Steven loved Jamie. Steven was devastated. Steven was enraged. He was in grief. He was unhinged. He blamed himself. He wanted to be heard. Maggie saw it all now. Now that it was becoming real.

He picked up another cookie and ate it carefully. It was the kind with a dot of jam in the middle. He ate the plain dough around the edges and saved the jam center for the end. He liked those cookies. He'd bought them for himself. Maggie was getting the picture. Brinkley took care of himself and others. Cookies for him and for her. He had a sense of other people's needs.

"So, what did you do?"

"I waited for Jamie to say something, to explain, to object, to do something. But when she didn't, it became clear to me that this was a normal part of her life."

"Her father barging in in the middle of the night."

"Exactly. So I asked him to leave. He seemed surprised, but went quietly. I assume people throw him out all the time."

"But not his daughter."

"Exactly." The memory of Jamie's reaction disturbed him, still. "I looked at her after the door closed and she was numb. Flat affect. Her lower lip was slack. Then she seemed confused. We started talking and I quickly recognized that she had no idea that this relationship with her father was . . ."

"What did she say?"

"Jamie said . . ." He was choked up now. He was still shocked. His voice trembled. He was retelling it, the truth. "She said, 'What do you want me to do? Pretend? *It's been this way my whole life.*'" He drowned. "She was used to it."

Maggie watched as Brinkley lost many years and gained many years. It was the recollection of how traumatized the life of the person you loved truly was. The drama of taking in the pain of a disappeared person, long after they're gone.

"I was kind," he said. "I stayed calm. I wanted to help her and my tone became . . . explanatory. I said that he was hurting her, and she . . ."

"Exploded in anger."

"Yes. How did you know?"

"Nothing makes people hate you more than the truth that can save their lives," Maggie whispered.

"Unless they want to know." He was bargaining still, to the grave.

"Did she want to know?"

"No. It was terrible, a failure. She started making crazy allegations. Blaming me for all of her pain."

Maggie didn't move. Just as Brinkley was living in the present and the past, so was she. Just as he was reliving the moment of doom that created the hell that now would be his life, so was she.

Brinkley kept talking but Maggie wasn't listening. She was back in her bed in her home with her lover and Frances was trying to stay calm, trying to be heard.

"Maggie," Frances said. "I love you. You are hurting me."

"Don't tell me what to do," Maggie hissed. She was livid. She wanted to kill Frances. No one who loved someone talked to them like that. Saying, "You're hurting me," that's not love.

"You're sick." Frances was crestfallen.

How dare she be crestfallen if she loved her? No one who was loved was disappointing! "Get away from me,

Frances. You're the drunk." Like there was only room for one. "Get away."

"You're ruining everything," Frances said.

No one who loved someone said, "You're ruining everything." That wasn't love.

"I don't care," Maggie said.

"You have to care. We're together. We have a child."

Now, watching Steven Berkley weep in another lifetime, it was so hard to remember what she was really thinking. She had wanted Frances to stop complaining. Was that it? To say that something very wrong was actually okay. She wanted Frances to shut up and go to Al-Anon or something that would make her stop nagging Maggie about her drinking. Actually, what was clear now, two years later, was that Maggie's number one desire had been for Frances to shut up so that she could drink and nothing else mattered. But at the same weird time, in some deeply denied way, in that exact same moment, Maggie realized that she had also really cared. That was the disease. She could see that now. She just was not able to take the chance to change, to be wrong. To not explode, to not accuse, to not position herself as a victim of abuse because her lover told her that she had to be reliable. That she had to be fair. Maggie had always handled everything with fire. And now she had ashes. Despite having felt two things at once, looking back at that key moment in their bed, together, in their brown sheets, in their bedroom, in their shared life with their beautiful child, Maggie Terry just couldn't figure out how to be accountable and survive.

CHAPTER ELEVEN

11:00 PM

Maggie was sweating and Steven was pale. There was an unsynchronized suffering, the contours of which were evident. Steven Brinkley was another Frances.

"Yes?" He was exhausted.

"What did you do?"

"When?"

"When you realized that the woman you loved, the young promising actress whom you believed would one day have success and financial security on her own, so that you two could move in together, someday. The one with whom you were careful to not breed dependency, but when her father was exploiting her, you stood up for her and then she made you pay. That woman. When you realized that she was sick . . ."

"Well . . ." Brinkley was stymied or hesitant or confused. "I feel . . ."

"Guilty?" Why couldn't Frances feel guilty? She was also a little guilty and that is not the same as innocent.

"I feel like smoking a cigarette."

"It's your beautiful townhouse."

Secretly, she doubted he would actually smoke. There was no scent of cigarettes in the air. There were no ashtrays or matches or lighters. Then she wondered if she wanted a cigarette. Had she ever really wanted one? Or was it just a time waster in between highs? She tried to imagine smoking.

"I feel like it, but I won't do it. What would be the point?"

She had been right but that was an intriguing comment, smoking for a *point*. Functional man.

He got up and went over to the stereo. He still had records. Did this man ever part with anything? Instead of walking away from the things and people the world had abandoned, he took care of them. Enjoyed them. He gave them value. She watched the way he handled these well-loved records, in excellent condition, and a pristine, well-loved turntable.

"Nothing sounds as good as a record."

"Is that really true?"

"No." He laughed, always unwilling to bullshit. "If you have expensive machines and headphones, the new technologies are better. But if you are listening on your iPhone . . ."

"How much are they?"

"Turntables?"

"No, iPhones."

He thought she was joking. "Funny." And then he put on John Coltrane's *Blue Train*, of course. Exactly what a rich, white, sensitive, middle-aged man with impeccable taste and a depth of feeling would play. "I guess . . ." he faltered. The music emerged. It was too loud. He lowered it. It was too low. "It's very hard to accept . . ."

"That she's dead?"

Steven began a sigh that became a whimper and could have turned to a wail if he hadn't restrained himself for her sake.

"That too. But honestly, I am not there yet. I was referring to the fact that she was mentally ill. That she had . . . conflicts . . . emotional conflicts and they were hurting her life. I mean, we all have emotional conflicts. I am not implying anything about my own superiority or purity."

"I understand."

"It's just that I saw her suffering and loved her and wanted to encourage her to do the work to feel well."

"Sometimes you can't fix it."

"Well, they always tell you that, but"—another cookie—"in fact, people make each other's lives better all the time, if we let them." He ate it like he was eating straw.

"So, what was your plan?"

"The first thing was to get Jamie into real therapy and far away from the Devil."

"Her father?"

He laughed. "I guess you don't know about Florence." Steven went to his huge carved dark-wood desk, large enough for two computers and a stack of books. "Here." He handed over a business card.

Dr. Florence Black
Healing Through Wishes

"She's a quack 'energy counselor' that Jamie was seeing. A failed actress, of course. I told her point blank that she needed to be in *real* therapy for sexual abuse and depression and Jamie's reaction was to—"

"Cut you off."

"Why, yes." He looked surprised.

Why was he surprised? No one wants to be told that their suffering is not caused by the people they are blaming it on.

"Jamie stopped taking my calls. I'd phone and phone and finally she picked up and yelled, 'You're sick. I'm going to call the police!' She acted like I was hurting her, but the bitter truth is"—Brinkley was so bitter, his lips seemed to dry and split—"that Jamie *was* being persecuted. But, not by me. By her schizophrenic father. Not by me!" He was insistent. It had wounded him, this accusation. "Florence stood by and did nothing. She let Jamie blame me for pain I had not caused. And now my poor girl is dead."

The doorbell rang.

"Excuse me, it's my Whole Foods delivery."

Maggie looked at her watch. "Can I use your phone?"

"Of course."

Once he stepped out of the room, Maggie dialed the old-fashioned landline, a push-button telephone in perfect condition. Expecting a recording, she was surprised to hear a person actually answer.

"Hello?"

"Oh, I'm so sorry to call so late. I was expecting your answering service."

"No, you got me. Can I help you?"

"Yes, I would like to make an appointment."

Ten minutes later, Steven returned with two bottles of what he explained to be kale juice, offering her one like it was a Heineken.

"Kale juice. I see it everywhere," Maggie said.

"Carrot juice is just sugar. Tamari almonds?"

She took an almond. It was salty and sweet. If she ate any more she would be drinking kale juice to wash them down. Is that something she really wanted to do? It was very late. Time for getting home and taking a shower and drinking hot water like she did every night, and would continue to do until she finally remembered to buy some tea bags.

"I'm tired." She handed back the business card.

"Don't you need that for your investigation?"

"Okay, thanks." She made a show of putting it in her pocket.

"Would you like to have a late dinner somewhere?"

That came out of nowhere. He had tried to deliver the invitation with a casual quality, like it didn't matter and didn't mean anything and nothing would come of it. Just eating. But these two human shadows were so endangered that nothing could happen between them without implication.

Maggie understood. He could smell her loneliness. Or else was too lonely himself to care. It was the blond hair. It was always the blond hair that they saw, but this guy also craved the damage.

"I'm so sorry. I have to go." She watched the sadness in his face, the slack shame of having his one and only plan for redemption thwarted by someone else's whim. No point in using her homosexuality as an excuse. She didn't know what role it played in her present bare existence, but she did know the history of her heart. "Listen," she said with mercy. "You don't want to go out with me. It will just be more of the same. You need to change your type. Find someone who can work things out. You know, an equal."

CHAPTER TWELVE

11:55 PM

On the thankfully air-conditioned 1 train home, people were tired. They were forgiving. They were thinking. They remembered and were exhausted by the memory. They shuffled and wished. The train rocked; its lights were bright. The seats provided a respite. Alone together. All of them were at the end and at the start of the day. They shared that.

Maggie and Julio had covered a lot of crimes that took place on the subway. An Arab woman was pushed in front of the 7 train. Her family wept and wept. They had come all the way to America for this? Every week or so someone jumped. The jumpers had an interesting psychology. They viewed the subway as part of the mechanics of the city itself. They didn't see it as tired, hardworking, and underpaid people having to clean up mangled torsos and severed heads while the rats feasted on their boiling blood. In their pain, they depersonalized their fellow New Yorkers and made the A train into a roving hospice, only there to serve their suffering. Subways were also for stabbings. Shootings during robberies or murder between friends. Lots of overdoses. People were using because they had no work, because they had too much work, because they were on their way to look for work, or because they hated work. And then she remembered that conductor who sold little bags of dope from station to station out of the window of the motorman's cab.

Maggie hauled her own carcass up the station's steps, emerging onto the concrete where those steps always lead. There was a light rain, not threatening. No need to react. She walked home, lost in her own throbbing sadness, finding her body leading her somewhere. Where was she going? Suddenly, she looked up and saw an unfamiliar row of wooden planks hammered over broken plate-glass windows. It was confusing . . . What? It did not compute.

And then she realized . . . that Georgie's Bar was gone. It had shut down, recently. And in its place sat another dark, empty storefront. Her unconscious had brought her to a drink that was no longer an option.

Maggie stepped into the new expensive Asian/Alsatian fusion restaurant next door with an unpronounceable name. Loud pop music she couldn't recognize, the lights too dim. No seeing, no hearing, no thinking, communicating, or feeling. The hostess awaited, menu in hand.

"Hi, excuse me."

"Just one? I can sit you at the bar."

"I have a question. What happened to Georgie's next door?"

"Lost their lease. The rent went up."

Very pretty, this young woman. Very correct, a sophisticated black woman, severe, too good for this job.

"Sad."

"Yes, but, they were a nuisance anyway." Jay-Z came on the sound system. "None of the businesses on the block cared for them. Wrong crowd. Can I seat you?" She was probably going to business school during the day.

Maggie looked over at the bar. It was inviting. The stools had backs, the drinks were tall. There were long exotic snakes laid out in tinted glass. Small batch bourbons from Kentucky, the kind that taste like slippery elm and oak and enlivened the soul. But what was that on the television? Trump in a wrestling arena, approaching the ring. One of the fighters was a cartoon figure with a CNN logo posted to his skull. Trump punched him repeatedly in the head. What was that? The president of the United States of America had tweeted this to the world. The world was confused. The world needed a drink. When was the last time Maggie had sipped good alcohol for the sake of taste instead of getting blotto? Maybe not for decades. Would Trump make her drink? No one would know.

"Thanks," Maggie said, heading toward the bar, like it was the easiest and most natural move in the world. That slide onto the stool. The gleaming bottles, their gorgeous sizes, the colors of the glass. The way bourbon was warm and tequila looked cool. The lovely ladies with their low-cut dresses, and catching the bartender's eye—and then panicking, pivoting, and running out the front door, back onto the street where it was really raining now. She had no protection. That wasn't a close call, she assured herself, stepping into the messy night. That was okay, she lied, back on the sidewalk that lay between her and safety.

The neighborhood had become boring. There were still some poor people there and some working-class people, but for the most part it was generic rich kids and the worst gay men. There was something reassuring about the blandness. Being cool was impossible. These people did drugs inside their apartments. They texted their dealers and the doormen let them in. Less temptation. Less opportunity. Less danger. People, Places, and Things. Stay away from People, Places, and Things if you want to stay sober. That's what they say in Program. *Stay away.* She was so far away. She was lost. How much more away could one person be?

Maggie's hair was soaking now. She looked like an idiot. Turning the corner to her street, she noticed a man standing alone in the doorway of someone else's expensive ground-floor apartment. He was standing out of the rain. He, too, looked miserable. His eye caught hers; he didn't care who knew. He lit his pipe. She saw the glow. He stared. There was no safe space. Not inside and not out. She rushed past him, stomping through the puddles, made a point to hold her breath.

Finally, Maggie made it to her front door and entered the hallway with her key like she was supposed to. Everything was a mockery, her ruined shoes. There was something she was supposed to attempt before ringing for the elevator. What do people do when they come home from work and stand in their own lobby? Something was missing. Oh yeah, pick up the mail.

Maggie wasn't expecting anything; she didn't have any subscriptions and letters no longer exist. But she had a mail key, and there might be a bill or a notice about the plumbing or something. She found her apartment's assigned box, turned the key in the tiny lock, and opened its little door. Nothing. Then she sloshed to the elevator, rang the bell. Tense, anxious, desperate, she waited, watching the light as it passed down five flights to her wet, drowned, hopeless emptiness. She kept going back to the man lighting his pipe. His lack of shame. Would he still be there? Would she be able to score? There was a moment of silence, then, inside, where all was suspended, she inhaled. Held the air. Until a hand landed on her shoulder, and she screamed.

Fingers clamped onto her skeleton and then released.

"I'm sorry," a man's voice murmured, filled with regret at his own actions. But it was too late.

Maggie lost control of her fear. She leaped back, hit the wall, turned to face her assailant, and then reached for the missing gun that she was no longer allowed to carry or own. Grasping again at nothing, she knew she was done. She would lose. Braced for the shot, the stab, the rope around her neck, the penis down her throat, she looked up, staring right into Steven Brinkley, also dripping rain, standing before her in the lobby of her own building. He was the man who had followed her home.

Not only was Maggie terrified at the threat standing before her, but she realized that her professional instinct was in a state of severe malfunction. She had been wrong about him. Dead wrong. This wasn't a nice guy. He was dangerous. He was a liar and a killer. Jamie was right; he was a stalker.

"I'm so sorry, I just had to talk to you."

The elevator arrived.

"Call me at the office, how did you get this address?"

The elevator door opened.

"Maggie, I have to talk to you, I feel so guilty. I feel so guilty. I should have tried harder."

Maggie backed into the elevator.

"I should have tried harder," he was weeping. "Please help me."

She pressed three.

He was fully sobbing, hopelessly wiping off his suffering with his hands. "Why did I let Jamie hurt me? She's sick. Why couldn't I understand that?"

The door closed. She could see his tortured face through the window, contorted with pain.

"Why?" he sobbed. "Why?"

The elevator departed. She was stunned. Anyone could find her. She could not hide; she could not protect herself. She was in danger at all times. She was weak and stupid and . . . The elevator stopped at three.

Maggie stepped out and ran toward the stairs. She looked down the corridor, listened closely to be sure that no one was coming, and then quietly went up two more flights, making sure that her footsteps no longer tracked water. On the fifth floor, she exited, called for the elevator. It arrived empty. She took it down one story to four, leaned out of the box. Empty. She walked slowly down her hallway and then slid into her bleak room. Something like Jamie Wagner's room, but without the fold-out couch.

Maggie trembled in the dark. Keeping the lights off, she stepped softly to the window and looked out through a tear in the newspapers Rachel had taped to the glass in lieu of the curtains Maggie was supposed to get to take care of herself. The street was covered in rain, and she saw no one. He seemed to have gone, but one could never be sure. She dragged some still-unpacked boxes over to barricade the door. There was so much grief in her heart; she was nothing but grief. Alone, because she was stupid, and in danger because she was alone, and stupid because she was herself. There was just no one to talk to. No place to share the reality of her stupid, stupid fate. Maggie fell to the floor, because she had to go somewhere. It was devastating, not knowing how to get out of this pit of terror. She wished, she wished, she found herself wishing for one thing. She needed one thing. If she could have anything, just one thing in the entire past or future, she knew what it would be. Maggie Terry staked all her dreams on the deepest dream she could find in her heart, the wish that she could have a beer.

DAY TWO

THURSDAY, JULY 6, 2017

CHAPTER THIRTEEN

7:OO AM

When the morning church bells rang at seven, Maggie was still lying on the floor in her damp, now-rancid outfit. She pulled everything off and threw the clothes in a corner, took a shower, still without a shower curtain, and then dried herself with the balled-up, filthy, wet laundry. She pulled out something too feminine that Rachel had purchased and hung in her closet. Then she ran to Nick's Deli.

"Maggie, you look great!" He applauded. "Did you go to the gym? You have color!"

"Not yet. Hi, Joe." She waved at Nick's assistant busy stocking shelves.

"Good morning." He waved. His English was improving.

This was going to be her most constant relationship. The person who knew day by day what she was supposed to be doing, a tiny chance to be accountable.

"Don't put it off. You'll end up skinny like me." He patted his enormous gut, barely contained by an egg salad–stained apron. "Listen, you don't want to look at the *Times* today, the news is very scary. Those people in Washington, they're out of their minds. Gives you indigestion."

"Thanks for the warning. One mint tea, one apple, one tabloid please."

"Good girl." He held up the *Daily News*. The headline held a jarring photo of Orange yelling "I'M PRESIDENT AND YOU'RE NOT."

"Uhm." Maggie felt anxious. "Do I have to?"

"Good call, I'll give you the *Post*. They like to pretend it's not happening."

She clutched the cup, wondering if she preferred mint tea. Or did it matter? Did she have to *like* what she drank each morning in order to anchor some kind of existence? Or was that even, as Steven Brinkley would say, *the point*? More important was to create some kind of stability, regardless of how it made her feel. So, drinking something that she wasn't sure she wanted, as long as it became a ritual, was the way to replace all the bad habits. New habits replacing old. And then she realized that once more she was starting *again* because it was another day, and she felt lighter, somehow. And then, she remembered that Brinkley knew where she lived, and shuddered.

Outside, Maggie watched every street, and checked over her shoulder, but he wasn't shadowing her. She made it to the meeting fairly sure that he was not on her tail. Maybe he was sleeping it off. Maybe he was writing a book about it. Climbing up the church steps, she realized she still had not tasted the tea nor bitten the apple, and had no desire to do either. So, clutching her two replacement crutches, she walked into Saint Peter's Greek Orthodox Church, stepped through the quiet dark hallway, and then took another set of interior stairs to the basement below.

It was the playroom of the Greek school's nursery program. From eight to nine the children had their breakfast in the church's kitchen so the grown-ups could wail and moan, blame and progress. These walls were covered in Greek flags, finger paintings, a crucifix. Blocks with imprinted English and Greek letters, storybooks in both languages. An enterprising young teacher had posted photos of Greek poverty interspersed with ancient ruins, the Parthenon next to the contemporary landscape of Greek chaos, angry demonstrators, cities in disrepair, unemployed people with nothing to do, refugees falling off of dilapidated ships, displacement camps, all juxtaposed with the startling blue jewel of the Aegean. The world of a four-year-old. Maggie stared at a cage of gerbils running in their creaking wheels. How appropriate.

In time to do service, she started pulling folding chairs off the rack laid out by the custodian for the addicts, and herding them into a circle. It was the only physical labor she did during the day, lifting and unfolding and then refolding cheap chairs. Other folks entered in varying emotional states, mostly in business drag or headed for some kind of job. Who else would go to an 8:00 a.m. meeting? Unless it was someone who'd stayed up all night crying and hauled their ass in before the temptation of bars opening at noon. Most unemployed would definitely sleep in. When there was nothing to do, time wasters are precious commodities, and sleeping in forever was the best way to stay away from drugs. They could dream about drugs. That might be better than being awake.

As the facilitator read through the standard summations and the twelve steps were passed around, Maggie retraced all her moves the previous night. Brinkley must have followed her down Perry Street to the 1 train.

1. We admitted we were powerless over alcohol—that our lives had become unmanageable.

He must have hung back and swiped his MetroCard at the last minute,

2. Came to believe that a Power greater than ourselves could restore us to sanity.

and then jumped on the same subway car,

3. Made a decision to turn our will and our lives over to the care of God, as we understood Him.

hiding down at the other end.

4. Made a searching and fearless moral inventory of ourselves.

He must have gotten out at her station, lurked along the platform,

5. *Admitted to God, to ourselves, and to another human being the exact nature of our wrongs.*

through the exits and up the stairs.

6. *Were entirely ready to have God remove all these defects of character.*

And he must have followed her in the rain.

7. *Humbly asked Him to remove our shortcomings.*

He also had no umbrella.

8. *Made a list of all persons we had harmed and became willing to make amends to them all.*

Hanging back, he'd accompanied her on her thwarted bar hop to Georgie's corpse and seen her almost sit down at the upscale froufrou place, planning which small-batch bourbon she was not going to consume.

9. *Made direct amends to such people whenever possible, except when to do so would injure them or others.*

He definitely saw her glance longingly at the man smoking crack on the street.

10. *Continued to take personal inventory and when we were wrong, promptly admitted it.*

He must have noticed which was her mailbox.

"It's your turn."

"What?"

The woman beside her handed Maggie the plastic-encased list of the twelve steps.

"Oh, I'm sorry."

"Number eleven," she whispered.

Maggie looked down, and then she read out loud, "Eleven. Sought through prayer and meditation to improve our conscious contact with God, as we understood Him. Praying only for knowledge of His will for us and the power to carry that out." She handed the paper to the man on her left.

What a joke. She could not be further from the eleventh step than from flapping her wings and flying to the moon. *Meditation?* She wasn't even listening to the meeting. Why was she coming here, if she let the cacophony of repetition in her mind distract her from getting better? *Let?* It wasn't that she *let* it. It was that she *used* it to avoid facing herself.

"Twelve," the skinny man next to her, reeking of tobacco, read with a husky grief. "Having had a spiritual awakening as a result of these steps, we tried to carry this message to alcoholics and to practice these principles in all our affairs."

But by the time they went around the room with introductions and she said, "My name is Maggie and I am a drug addict and an alcoholic," and everyone else greeted her, "Hi, Maggie," like it was a Gregorian chant of transcendence, she knew in her heart that while Steven Brinkley was a creep, and while he was a strategist, a sneak, a liar, a predator, and a manipulator, he was absolutely not a killer because she was still alive. In the end, after all that trouble, he had let her get away. And someone who could strangle a young woman to death could strangle a middle-aged one as well.

Andrew H., a white businessman, was giving his qualification. His mother blah blah blah, the confusion, the drinking at age twelve, etc., etc., etc., the lying, the self-destruction, the hiding. All the cars he had crashed, all the people he had fucked over, but he was fine *now*. That was the point. That was the point sometimes of these qualifications. *You* could fuck people over and still come out on top. *You* could be Andrew H., with a wedding ring and a great suit. Maggie looked around the circle. How many of these people had done terrible things to others who had already overlooked or forgotten whatever elaborate transgression had been orchestrated by the deviousness of their disease? If you just get better, do the people you hurt get better, too?

Then there was Martha L., a fortysomething black woman with a short, graying, natural hairstyle in exquisite corporate clothing. Impeccably pressed. Martha's life might be a raging torment, but she looked fabulous. She knew how to shop and how to take care of her clothes, even while she had them on. She knew how to avoid getting them stained or even wrinkled by the banalities of daily life. She was a perfectionist. Martha could have held any position in any office from CEO to receptionist, but she would always be the best dressed. Next to speak was Ramón, a Latino maintenance man, early forties, in his company-issued jumpsuit, and a logo, *Freeways* with a fish happily wielding a mop. He could have been in anything: aquarium, plumbing, parole. Whatever he cleaned, and whomever he cleaned up after, Ramón wore his uniform out on the street as proof of identity. He was doing okay, *today*. It was all about today.

The smoker to her left was revealed to be Bashar. And he had problems that were larger than his own cravings.

"I am from Qatar. I am so worried, so worried. My family. A forty-eight-hour deadline. I am so scared. Thank you."

Then, Susannah, a white mom, capital M-O-M, was trying to get a real estate license. She wanted a social role outside of Mommyland and seemed to hate her husband and resent her kids. Her fantasy was that with her "communication skills," or something, she would be able to "break into" real estate in New York City. The entire city was a safe deposit box for the richest people in the world, everyone knew that. Money launderers—possibly including the president—were buying multimillion-dollar apartments in cash. How was this chick going to *break in? Break down* was more likely when she realized that there was no way out of hating her own family. She was going to have to love them or crack up entirely. But maybe she wanted to fail, Maggie realized. Maybe, that's why she had given herself an impossible goal, so she could end up having another child and continue avoiding the problems that made her feel so bad. Supposedly, if the Program worked, a person could end up loving themselves no matter what they did for a living, or who they were related to. The family situation will improve, the Program boasted. But at the cost of what? Of justice?

Next was Ronald, a student, who was one of those buff Asian good-old-boy, all-American types who wore shorts over their gym pants. He carried an NYU travel mug. He just wanted to stay sober. No matter what. Then there was Scott, a young white businessman; Omar, a middle-aged Arab guy dressed in clean, well-fitting jeans—could have been gay. Charles, another white businessman, spoke next—he could have been sober for thirty years but alcoholism had taken its toll. He was constantly licking his lips, glancing about, and looking uncomfortable in the world. Next to him, Carlos, an older Latino executive type; Steven, a weathered black man who seemed absolutely miserable; Monica, a washed-out loser who seemed high; Katrina, a Russian model or would-be model, that was unclear. There was Sheila, an Italian American middle-aged secretary with a mustache who had barely made it out of bed. And on.

"And, here I am," Joseph was finishing his three-minute share. "Today, triumphant. Thank you." Another one of *those*. Maggie rolled her eyes, and then felt ashamed. Who was she to judge?

Everyone clapped, some with enthusiasm and hope that someday they would have the spouse, the good job, or just feel the love that was already there. They were all trying their best, and Maggie was not. That was evident, and she had to admit that they inspired her. Maggie raised her hand and in a miraculous act of mercy, Joseph called on her.

"My name is Maggie and I am an alcoholic and an addict."

"Hi, Maggie."

"Hi, everyone. Thank you for your service."

She always said that because somehow this was the aspect of sharing at a meeting that impressed her the most: that telling other people the truth was "service." Nowhere else on earth was this the case. For most people the telling of the truth was worse than the awful truth itself.

"Today is my second day of work sober. Ever. I've been through detox and rehab, court, a halfway house, and I have been trying to live on my own for one week now. I . . . lost my child."

This was the moment when she was supposed to say how she felt. How do you do that? Keep It Simple was the slogan. Don't tell the long story. As a police detective, she knew that the truth lay in the details. She could hear Julio say it over and over again. What was the order of events? What was the originating action? What were the consequences? What did each person do and why did they do it? What did they hope would be the outcome? And most importantly, *what was the actual outcome?* But here, in 12 Step–land, somehow that wasn't supposed to matter. The specificity, where the truth lay, was not important. It was the simplicity; it was through the looking glass. Because in Program they were not trying to figure out who was going to get punished.

How do I feel?

She felt afraid. She wasn't afraid of Steven Brinkley. But she couldn't explain all that in a three-minute share. No, he wasn't going to be the one to hurt her, that was a fact. What scared Maggie was that she had gotten rattled so fast. That, sober, she had no more cool to lose. It was gone, the foolish bravado that she was untouchable. What was she supposed to do? Find a way to get foolish bravado out of mint tea, or find a way to be terrified all the time and let that be okay? Sobriety was all about disappointing choices between flawed options. Could that really be . . . life?

"I am scared."

Some of the folks nodded. They lived to identify. When other people felt bad, sometimes that gave them hope that they could feel better. Each of them lived to be forgiven.

"That's all I want to say. Thank you."

Hands shot up. She was lost in a swirl of pain. Everyone was staring. Was she really that much of a freak? The whole room was looking right at her with desperate neediness and their hands above their heads. What had she said that was so objectionable and urgent?

"It's your turn to call on someone," muttered Bashar, the forlorn young student from Qatar. He had wasted his own share on how much he didn't want his country bombed because a greedy, impulsive ignoramus was president of the United States. That wasn't going to keep him sober.

It was not a group wave. It was her responsibility to call on the next speaker. Maggie chose mousy Monica, who seemed to be on the nod.

At the end of the meeting, Maggie picked up her now-cold mint tea and finally took a sip. She still couldn't tell if she liked it. Was it bitter? Was that bad? She held the apple. It was so unattractive and had nothing to give. The red looked fake, and it felt mealy in her hand. She picked up her purse, placed the apple in her bag, continued to grip the tea like it was the propulsion handle on a jetpack, and started toward work. At the top of the stairs, through the dark hallway, now filled with squealing Greek children, all of whom understood that they were *sooooo* lucky to be in America and not back home where there was no food, stood Omar, knapsack over one shoulder, waiting for her with the door held kindly open.

"I've been there and I know how hard it is," he said softly. Slight accent. "You're worth it. Just keep coming back."

"Thanks. Omar, right?"

"Yeah. Do you have a sponsor? It really helps."

"Yeah." He was doing service. "Rachel. She's a lifesaver."

"Good. You can't miss."

"I'm so lonely." There, she'd finally said it. "Facing myself."

He smiled very warmly, seemed to be a kind of relaxed professional. Maybe a college professor. "Just stay around Program people for a while. It makes a difference."

"I wish sober people went to bars."

"There is a Program dance tonight at Saint Luke's."

"Dance? I've never danced sober. I can't even imagine it." Dancing is all about sex, and sex is all about . . .

He smiled. She looked for a wedding ring. He must be gay. The ring Frances had given her was rolling around her finger. Their relationship was long ended and Frances had gotten married to someone else, but Maggie had never taken it off. Yet. And her finger was smaller or thinner now, or else that ring was trying to get away from her, too. Gay people wear wedding rings these days. Frances was wearing one, when Maggie had last seen her, which was in court. She looked at her own ring. She twirled it with her right hand. No, she just couldn't take it off. That ring meant Alina.

"I know you can," Omar said.

CHAPTER FOURTEEN
9:10 AM

Craig was waiting for her outside the church, just as he had promised. Now that they were out on the street together, his lack of height and the girth around his middle were both a lot more prominent. Apparently, he was reliable, despite his constant displays of irritation. He paced, mumbled, showing in all possible ways his desperation to get every show on the road. He was the kind of person who walked up the stairs deciding exactly what he was going to do when he got to the top. I will turn left, then check my phone, straighten my tie, and then turn right. It made it all make sense. He needed to understand what came next, and when the road was clear, only then could he advance. Maggie saw that as hurried and overburdened as he seemed to always be, Craig was never, ever late. This contributed to his general state of annoyance, which scampered before him, like a puppy. People who are *always* on time consider it a sign of decency, based on the principle of keeping their word. Saying "I will meet you at nine" is a promise, something the promised can rely on, and in turn they are then free to make and keep promises to others predicated on everyone being predictable. I can meet you at 9:10, because Craig is meeting me at 9:00 was the imagined domino effect he craved and was so proud to be a part of.

"It's ten after nine," he spat.

He was hurt, she could see it. Her lateness told him that she had not taken him into account, while he had fully considered her.

"Sorry."

He was insulted, put-upon already, and it was not even 9:15. "You should have texted."

"I'm sorry," she said. "I'm sorry that I am ten minutes late, and I am sorry that I didn't think to text you, and I am sorry that even it if had crossed my mind I wouldn't have been able to, because I still don't have a cell phone, and I haven't even checked to see if the landline is working because, I am sorry, I forgot about it." Was she sincere? Did it matter right now? Better to get in the habit, and maybe taking responsibility would become part of her new life.

He stared at her.

"I am very, very sorry, Craig, and this is all entirely my fault."

Maybe the Program was working. She didn't have to hide in a bottle. She could just say it.

"Here."

He handed her a bunched-up plastic bag, the kind that ecologists know kill birds, but that people use anyway for some unquantifiable reason.

"Is this trash?"

"Open it."

"Now?"

"YES, NOW!" He hit his palm on his forehead and looked to the sky. She could see him mouth the words *Praise Jesus.*

Inside the bag was a little red flip phone, the kind that an eleven-year-old might carry, or maybe some kind of burner. In fact, since it had no packaging, it probably had belonged to one of his children who now were in possession of a far more sophisticated piece of technology.

"I programmed my number."

"Thank you, Craig. That is very, very sweet." Her Higher Power had partnered with a control freak to help make her minimally functional. And she realized that for the rest of her tenure at Fitzgerald & Robbins, which could be a matter of minutes unless one miraculous morning she woke up perfect, Craig Williams would be correcting her, fixing her. He would be right up her ass.

But, she did know enough to understand that he did this for himself. He just wanted to be able to find her. It wasn't sweet, it was just practical. He'd probably grown up with a disorganized parent and had to wash his own towels from before he was old enough to take the subway by himself. He had to control in order to survive, and in fact, her lack of responsibility in the face of this was doubly pathetic. But if she wasn't capable of buying tea bags, how would she ever figure out how to get a telephone? So, despite it all being highly dysfunctional, it was a good thing he was controlling her. It helped.

Craig started walking toward the office. "So, how did it go?"

She ran to stay within earshot. "Oh, the usual. Pain, resistance, self-deception, effort."

"No, the case!" Craig sighed. He'd had it.

Should she recount the long, tortured evening with Steven Brinkley? Keep It Simple.

"I have a lead. Jamie's therapist. I made us an appointment for this morning. Here is her card."

Craig took it and typed the address into his phone. "Seven blocks south," he reported.

She looked up. The street sign said Sixteenth. "Well, her office is on Ninth Street so that sounds about right."

Craig didn't even wince, that's how much she bothered him.

"What kind of effort?" he asked abruptly.

"To participate."

"In what?"

"The world."

"I get it."

He seemed interested. In fact, in his ever overly critical way, he was very supportive. Maybe she had been right about his parents, one dysfunctional and the other always compensating.

"I shared."

"What does that mean?"

"I told them about my problems."

They crossed the River Styx otherwise known as

135

Fourteenth Street—impervious to the chic and rife with chicanery—and descended into the calm of Greenwich Village, where the 1950s bourgeoisie had seized the nineteenth century from the impending claws of Jackie Bouvier–style boxy, white-brick buildings, guaranteeing calm side streets for the very private wealthy, even though they no longer had a hospital or any place to do the laundry or buy shoes or a hamburger that was under twenty dollars. For someone who lives in a fifteen-million-dollar brownstone, that may not matter, but even those people want to go for a walk amid the hoi polloi from time to time.

"Is that what goes on in there?"

"Yeah Craig, struggles and hopes."

"That keeps you sober?"

"So far."

Was he being deadpan or sincere? "If I had to listen to other people's problems day in and day out, I would need a drink."

"Everyone says that."

"Obvious, I guess."

"Yeah, only I need a drink even if I am not listening to anyone." Maggie coasted beside him. "That's the difference."

She filled him in about Florence, the hack shrink, condensing the report to Brinkley's description, not describing Brinkley much at all. Why was she protecting him? They turned off Sixth Avenue and down Ninth Street.

"Hard to believe this used to be cheap."

"Yeah." Craig nodded. "Hard to believe this whole city used to make sense."

Maggie thought back to the days before her days, of single lady poets and youngsters with acoustic guitars making their own way. People *ran into* each other, and ignited a collective leap forward. Now it was filled with people no one would want to be stuck with in an elevator.

"Here," he said, following his phone.

Feeling a familiar old itch, Maggie looked up and was startled by the building's facade. She had not expected to be back at this address so soon. Or ever.

"It's the shrink building." She had been there with Frances. Twice.

"Whatever."

"The whole building is filled with shrinks."

They had tried couples counseling with a stupid dyke who had no idea of how to talk to either of them. She would throw everything back, and they just didn't know what to do with it. It didn't help. They needed more guidance. They needed the shrink to be the boss. Their stuff was too tough and they needed to be told how to fix it. Then Frances got desperate and wouldn't just wait for a breakthrough; instead she changed her tune. She seemed to be getting advice from somewhere else, someone Maggie didn't know. Weird words would come out of her mouth, words Maggie had never heard before like *visual information* or *no, no, no* and wagging her finger. Someone else's voice was getting into Frances's head. Suddenly, one session, Frances walked in and said, "I want us to both drop these repetitive stories that we hide behind. No, no, no." She wagged her finger. "Let's use some visual information to help us through this, look at us! We are both wrecks. We have to come to a new understanding or someone could die around here."

"Die?" the therapist repeated, nervous it could be her.

"Maggie is a police detective. She is going to work drunk. Something terrible could happen."

Whoa, that was really playing dirty. What was Maggie supposed to say? This was a new gambit: that unless Frances got her way, someone was going to come in DOA.

"What do you suggest?" the therapist said, always throwing it back on them.

"We both need to stop drinking so that we can figure this out," and then Frances looked down at the floor, because it was *sooooo* obvious how manipulative she was being.

"That is *not* going to happen," Maggie said.

"Just try." Frances was pleading. Now, of course, Maggie realized that Frances had been lying. She now knew Frances had a plan B, named Maritza. But Maggie didn't know that at the time. So, really it was a *solution* used as a smoke screen for a threat. "We're here together, baby. Let's both adjust."

Her desperation made Maggie so uncomfortable, and she did not want to be uncomfortable. It was a trick, to make Maggie be the problem. If she conceded one little thing, then suddenly it would all be her fault. That's how those games were played. So, Maggie refused.

Finally, after a few expensive months they were both so exhausted from the struggle, they sat back for a while, overlooked it. Both hoped that the next time this pain came to a head, each of them would deal with it differently. But a few years later, things got hard again and someone referred them to another gray-haired Jewish doctor who turned out to be in the exact same building.

Shrink Number Two was a true disaster. Frances tried to tell Dr. Edith Rosenblatt that Maggie was a drug addict. So, Maggie told Dr. Edith Rosenblatt that Frances was a drug addict. Since the doctor's futile strategy was to not take sides, she simplistically said, "Let's not make accusations," instead of listening close enough to find out that Maggie was in fact an addict and that Frances was not. Bad doctor.

Craig scanned the names on the buzzers.

"There it is. Florence Black, Energy Counselor." He pressed the button. "Okay, here we go."

"Hey Craig, have you ever been to a shrink before?"

"No."

"Okay, just be yourself."

CHAPTER FIFTEEN

10:00 AM

Florence's waiting room was a cramped, depressing hallway with no windows and unwieldy wicker chairs that had never been comfortable, which is why they had been on clearance in the first place, decades past. Florence was a person who could not replace bad furniture as long as it wasn't broken. In her magazine rack was *Yoga Journal*, a year-old copy of *Psychology Today*, and an out-of-date edition of *Us Weekly* opened to the horoscope page.

Maggie looked at Alina's sign, Pisces. *Conflict will not resolve until your birthday.* Today was July 6. There were a lot of months ahead until February 22. Then she looked at Frances's, Leo. *Don't let another person's agenda interrupt your own.* Then Maggie looked at her own sign, Leo. *Don't let another person's agenda interrupt your own.*

"Craig, what's your sign?"

"Scorpio."

"Family members will come to stay."

"I know."

On the wall was a framed photograph of naked white children playing on the beach. They both stared at it.

"Something about thinking of one's self as innocent," Maggie mused.

"Off-putting," Craig said.

There was something interesting about Craig, beyond his disapproval of everything. What did he actually like?

"What do you like?"

"Chris Rock."

"Is that a joke?"

"He's not that bad. Whatever. What am I supposed to say? Who is the new PC black person we're all supposed to want to be? I'd say Obama, but that's like nostalgia for utopia."

"Do you ever think about starting your own firm?"

He nodded six times. "Twen-ty-four-sev-en."

There was something about that waiting room that made people so bored, they became disoriented. It provoked a desperate need for distraction. Presiding over the magazine rack, taped to the wall, was a small framed postcard with some saying on it, but the letters were too small to read. Maggie got up, walked over and read out loud, "What is most important is how you see yourself."

"Well, that's wrong." Craig was over everything about this office. "In fact, that attitude is *the* big problem. People only think about themselves, not how they are affecting others."

"Pretty deep."

"I have a family," Craig said casually, like it explained, excused, organized, and informed everything.

And Maggie was destroyed.

When Florence opened the office door flipping her one-shade-of-brown dyed hair with gray roots, in a billowy olive-green blouse and hideous necklace of what looked like dried cow ears but turned out to be shells, she found a devastated Maggie and a shut-down, angry Craig. A typical couple. She smiled, in the satisfaction of familiarity, and silently waved them into her office.

Inside, the decor revolved around a little electric waterfall, tumbling endlessly into a pool. A tired motor cycled the water up through a plastic tube so that it could come flowing down once again, and then again. The gears growled, crying out for upkeep.

"Please." She pointed to a battered couch underneath a large pink conch shell affixed to a faded white wall. "Take a seat."

Maggie sat first. The couch had been too soft for too long, so when Craig followed suit, the flattened cushions forced them into an intimate proximity.

"I can help you with your marriage." Florence lit two white candles and brought her hand to her heart. "If you wish it so."

Craig sighed, but Maggie didn't dismiss people that quickly. If Florence had managed to stay in business this long with such a clumsy setup, she must have something to say that felt meaningful to other people. It didn't have to be *a lot* of other people, just enough to pay the clearly stabilized rent. Maggie's job here was to listen closely and figure out what had felt so compelling to poor Jamie Wagner. What did Jamie need that Florence had? Or perhaps, more likely: What did Florence never say that kept Jamie coming back? After all, as Maggie eventually learned in rehab, therapists organize the therapy around what they think the patient can actually accept, not what they perceive to be true. In order to help them, the therapist has to create an environment the patient will not flee. And some people who are very, very hurt will flee at the first sign of a fact. So far Maggie did agree with Florence about one very important value: any conflict could be resolved if everyone wanted it to be resolved. If Frances wanted to solve this custody impasse, she could. But the problem was that she wanted *revenge*. She wanted to get back at Maggie over and over, day in and day out, for how much time she had wasted trying to get Maggie to really connect, really love. And that was why she wouldn't work it out now. The custody.

"Great," Craig said. "Because my wife Maggie here is tormented. She's depressed, shut down, can't handle basic life tasks, and is overall out of it."

Florence reached out and took both their hands.

"You can't communicate with each other, but you can communicate through me."

Maggie imagined Frances at the other end of this human chain of contact. If someone had done this with them, it would have helped.

"Maggie, what Craig just said, is it true?"

"No," Maggie replied. Just as she had said to Dr. Edith Rosenberg, Rosen*blatt*, whatever, so long ago. "No, Craig is the one who is sick."

Florence squeezed her hand, like a reminder, a reminder that she did not have to play it that way. She had choices, lots of choices. She had the choice to be a flawed person in the world of others who were in exactly the same boat. She didn't have to be right and she didn't have to blame and she didn't have to punish. She could heal instead.

"Honey." Craig was playing it to the hilt now. "I'm on your side." It was like he had been in this game before, somewhere, the games that people play to stay sick when they have a chance to get well. When they'd come all the way to couples counseling and only one person is there to negotiate, ready to give in and also to be given in to, while the other squanders every opportunity for change. "Maggie, your father is sexually invasive," he said. "I am not blaming you. I am blaming him."

Craig was good at his job. He had instincts. He wasn't just a tech wonk; he could smell a wound.

"No," Maggie said, like it was an obvious and classic case of gaslighting, yet another man trying to silence his wife by claiming that she was crazy. "It's *you*, Craig." Frances. "You are the cause of the problem. It's your fault."

Craig threw up his hands to illustrate his helplessness. Yes, Maggie was sure now. He had definitely been here before.

"See, Doc . . ."

"See what, Craig?"

"Can you see, Florence, that I don't know what to do?"

"Yes."

Florence closed her eyes. She brought her hands to her lips. She wasn't exactly praying, just waiting.

"Maggie," she said finally. "What do you wish?"

"I wish that Craig would stop saying anything that upsets me." That was the truth. It was the truth about Craig, about Frances, about every fucking doctor, cop, and social worker who had been in the way of her not changing her view of herself.

"How can the world leave you alone when you are in it?"

Ahhhhhhh.

"You, Maggie." Florence had a bland singsong quality. She was not a distraction. "You want Craig to stop *thinking* those things and *feeling* those things? You want to change his interior life? Or, do you just want him not to express what he feels and thinks, sees and understands. Do you want him to be controlled by your weaknesses? Or do you want him to be real?"

"He should fix himself," Maggie said. That was it, wasn't it? Everyone was blaming Maggie and no one was blaming themselves. But she didn't do all these bad things on her own. That would be impossible. There was the liquor industry, for one.

"Craig?"

"Huh?" Craig had been Craig and wandered off into his anxiety about what was waiting for him in his email.

"Craig," Florence said, and then she waited. "It is your job to make Maggie's wish come true."

"What?" Craig threw his hands up in disgust. Being

145

a short, rotund fellow made that hand-throwing thing rather animated. "You call this *therapy*? Making ridiculous demands that aren't going to help anybody?"

Florence smiled. This is exactly what she wanted from them: a reaction on her terms. "With six months of dream work I can make your wish come true, Maggie. Craig will stop saying things that upset you, and Craig, I can make your wish come true as well. Maggie will stop being upset by the things that you say."

"Okay." He got it. "You don't change what we do, you change how we feel about it, and then we don't need to do it because it won't have the same meaning."

Maggie had a moment of recognition here. How she was emotionally ricocheting between possible interpretations of moments because she was jumping from denial to acceptance and back to denial again. In a way, Florence was right, of course. Everyone, to some degree, had a choice about how to react. Frances might have been lonely and frustrated, she might even have been disappointed or afraid. But she didn't have to run off with a younger woman.

"Right." Florence smiled. Her method was working as she knew it would. "I can heal you by teaching you to be comfortable with difference, with acknowledging hard truths, with receiving love. We will all come together twice a week and listen to the sound of the waterfall, until we have memorized it, emotionally. Then, when someone else's truth feels unbearable, you substitute the sound of the flowing water."

Craig dropped his arm down, in surrender, and one hand splashed in the pool. Even back on the hot summer street his sleeve was still dripping wet.

"Oh my God," he said as they headed back to the office. "Two hundred dollars a session for that crap." He worked his device. "I bet she doesn't even have a license."

"Her *doctorate* is in Victorian literature," Maggie answered quietly, thinking.

"Hold on!" He waved his screen like it was a football after touchdown. "You're right. Her PhD is in . . . *Victorian literature*. How did you know that?"

"I looked on her bookshelf. The closest thing she had to a clinical text was Mary Shelley's *Frankenstein*."

"Whatever. What a clown."

But Maggie didn't agree. Jamie Wagner was an actress, after all. She memorized scripts that other people wrote. She did not originate ideas; she interpreted them. The kinds of assignments Florence handed out could work for someone who wanted to be told how to reason and respond. Someone desperate for another way. It could work for Jamie, provide a relief from never being able to figure it out on her own. Maggie imagined Florence instructing Jamie Wagner: The next time your father says something sexual to you, think of the sound of the flowing water.

It was an avoidance technique. You can't change other people so stop listening to them. No need to understand, just distract so that you can coexist. Right up Jamie's dissociated alley. She was internalized anyway. She did not need to be awake, just to act awake. But in Maggie's case, it was different. She was hyperaware, how could she ever just stop noticing. It was her sensibility and it was her profession. Seeing through other people's facades was what she did for a paycheck.

Except when it came to the mirror. But when she'd punctured Frances's facade, she'd punctured her heart because Frances needed to be the good guy. And if Maggie had just listened to the water circulating through a beat-up mini waterfall, she could have let it go.

Now there was no mirror, no badge, no institution of power, no apparatus of enforcement. She was, in all senses, a civilian. She could think of dirty water every time she missed her child. Was it really possible to never pay attention again? As a way of life?

"What do you say, Craig? Do you think you could give up noticing?"

But Craig was too busy with his email to even feign a reply.

CHAPTER SIXTEEN
11:30 AM

Maggie's office was a replica of her apartment. Empty.

The firm had provided a desk, a chair, and a gorgeous wall of windows for which curtains were only a necessity to the perpetually suicidal. The blank white walls and Spartan desktop were a regular and daily threat to any illusion of progress. What belonged there? Old photographs of Alina?

The fact was that Alina did not look like that anymore. She'd outgrown those clothes and lost that barrette. She was probably losing her baby teeth and had bangs and some kind of commercial sneakers and a new vocabulary and ran boldly without hiding behind her mother's legs. She had a lunch box with logos from a pop star or TV show that Maggie had never heard of and could not discuss. She played computer games that Maggie could not bear or understand. She had friends Maggie had never met, and dreams. What was the point of replaying that soft little hand, the way she would lean against Maggie's body like she owned it, the lack of self-consciousness—it was all probably gone.

And the questions . . . "Is that your little girl?"

"It was."

No, she couldn't bear it.

Yet Maggie could not move every day from one barren crypt to another and back again, with stop offs in dank church basements in between. There was something absurd about being in such an elaborate city only to be surrounded by emptiness. Outside and within.

She took out that tiny red cell phone and the phone number crushed in her wallet, and started trying to figure out how to enter Rachel into her contacts so that Craig would not be the only one for the police to call if she got hit by a car. Or if she was found with a needle in her arm, moldering underneath a staircase in Middle Village, Queens. Or if the inability to decorate finally seized her mind and she ended up naked on the escalator at Macy's.

There was a knock, but it turned out to be symbolic when her office door opened without any pretense of waiting for permission.

"Maggie?"

It was Mike of course. That would be his way around here. Facsimile of privacy, when we're all one big happy family. Well, she did not need more privacy; it would only get her in trouble. What was the difference between privacy and loneliness? A tree without leaves or a dead tree?

"Great day, isn't it?"

She had to look up then and notice the sun, the blue, the clarity, the distinction between cloud and universe.

"Yes, lovely."

Mike's role was to accentuate the positive. And hers was to try to receive it. He took a thick file of papers off of his lap and threw it on her empty desk. Now there was something on her desk.

"That oughta mess it up."

"Thanks!"

"It's the info you requested on Jamie's father. Guy's got a massive history of problems. We still xerox around here in case the internet disappears one day, and someone has to be left to sue them. I like the feel of paper, and it'll give you something to write on. You don't mind, do you?"

"No, the NYPD was all about paper."

"Good. Want you to feel at home."

"Thanks."

"And it gives you something to put in your brand-spanking new, empty, clean file drawers."

Barely a lonely breath after, the door slammed and she stared back out at the world through her window. It was daunting and anxiety provoking. She felt overwhelmed and afraid and so went back to trying to call Rachel. She knew she needed support. Something bad was going to happen, and Maggie needed her sponsor. But before she could make the thing dial, there were three short blasts on her intercom. This was Sandy's summons for a meeting in Mike's office that he hadn't mentioned ten minutes before, and so had probably just decided to call. Mike's persona, after all, was *spur of the moment* meets *right now!*

"So, everyone, Maggie has just been reading Jamie's father's files."

"Actually, I haven't even opened—"

"Got it!" Craig announced. "Stefan Wagner!"

The visit to faux couples counseling hadn't helped their relationship, that was for sure. He was still competitive.

Craig proudly read off his phone, "Born in Germany. Five involuntary hospitalizations by the police. Diagnosed severe manic-depressive. Lifetime of thought disorders. Electric shock."

Enid clapped her hands, helpless. "How in the world can you find out a person's most intimate tragedies in ten seconds?"

"Police records. Hospital records."

Enid shook her head. "That truly terrifies me. The problem with the world is too much informa—oh, wait. That was the problem with the world *before* the election. Now the problem is not enough *real* information. Half the people in this country are out of their minds."

"Actually," Craig droned. "Thirty-six percent."

"Is that that evil man's latest approval rating? I blame those Bernie Bros, it's all their fault. They splintered the Democrats and the crazies voted for a president who is going to take away their own health—"

"Okay," Mike said.

"I know," Enid whispered.

"We know."

"Anyway." Craig was back to business. "Stefan Wagner is a real mess."

"That," Maggie recalled, "was exactly how Steven

Brinkley described him." And she realized that Jamie's father and her boyfriend basically had the same name.

"And Brinkley was right about Florence Fake-o, too," Craig interjected. He caught Maggie's eye. "I know, I know, you *liked* her."

"I wouldn't go that far."

"Well." Enid took off her jacket. She seemed to be having hot flashes but had not yet said so. Still, everyone who noticed assumed as much, except for the men and those too young to consider such things. In other words, no one in that room but Maggie. "It is criminal," Enid continued, "that Jamie was never sent for psychopharmacological evaluation. Medication can really make a difference." She was sweating. "I took them for a short time when my second husband was convicted of embezzlement and they helped me."

"Wow." Craig was always embarrassed by other people.

Enid gulped down a glass of water. "I don't need them now."

"I am so glad." Mike patted her arm. "It's great to see you feeling better." He gestured around the room with his glasses. "We are all really glad."

Enid seemed to get chilled and put her jacket back on, then stared at Maggie, daring her to say the word *menopause*. "What about you?"

"I'm not on *anything*."

"But you were involuntarily hospitalized by your former domestic partner. Can you handle working on this case?"

Bitch.

"You were?" Craig was so surprised he didn't even look up, like he didn't want to be caught in a state of unknowing.

The pain came from the word *former*, carefully selected by Enid for maximum infliction, since she also had to live with that ghost.

"Maggie, we are all so glad that you are feeling better." Michael glared lovingly at Enid, clearly telegraphing that she had better take her hostility down a few notches. After all, he had been supremely understanding about her varieties of hormonal mood swings and aging-related outbreak/depression cycles.

"Yes," Maggie said, although she knew it was a lie. "I can take it." What was she supposed to say?

"How is Frances? And your little—"

"Michael, we aren't in touch right now."

"Oh, I'm sorry to hear that."

"Thank you."

She wasn't going to explain that Frances did that to her when everything happened with Julio, because frankly it was none of their business and they wouldn't understand. They wouldn't understand the Code. She knew everyone in America was watching police officers kill black people; it was part of the horror show/reality/ entertainment news update. People would watch and rewatch Eddie kill Nelson Ashford for no reason, but Maggie knew there was a reason that none of these people could understand. Yes, it was racism, okay, that was obvious. The police were afraid of black people, and that was a fact, because it was widely believed among police officers that black people hated them. And if any of the cops—brown and black cops especially—were civilians instead, they would hate the police, too. But once they put on that badge, blue became thicker than race. She'd seen it over and over again. Of course, the black cops were also black people, and some of them even got shot by a white officer for no reason when they were plainclothes or out with their kids or at the wrong picnic or something. But when Julio's son killed that man, Julio took the cop point of view.

"If Nelson Ashford had just listened to Eddie," Julio had cried in the car. "If he had just done what Eddie said, instead of stalling and asking questions and playing that *I'm protecting my rights* television cops-and-robber game, if he had just . . . *obeyed*, he would be alive today," Julio mourned. "That man would be alive today."

So, while Maggie knew that in the world of people having the right to go home from work without being killed, Nelson Ashford should not have been killed—obedience was not the solution to police violence—she also knew the world of junior, second-generation cops of color, who see everyone else as a threat, who feel the hate. They grew up with their fathers being treated like traitors, but being told that they were heroes. In that reversal world, Eddie Figueroa did what Julio Figueroa would have done. He shot first. And there was proof.

"It's driving me crazy, Maggie," Julio said. His soft brown skin was sagging under the weight of his heavy eyes. "I can't believe they put Eddie on leave. Charges, man! Charges. Those cowards."

"I know." Maggie coughed. "You're right."

Normally the force and the commissioner were

supposed to have the officer's back. But, what was Eddie doing there anyway? Outside of his beat? He said he was following a lead. He had a bullshit story that couldn't be confirmed or denied about a civilian waving down his car when he was headed back to the station and pointing him to a disturbance over by some small apartment buildings where some petty criminals lived. Well, every building in New York has criminals. Every New Yorker knows that. Rich or poor they are scamming something, whether it's Jared Kushner's slumlording, an old auntie's illegal dice game, or some young queen's sex work. Eddie could have had some fishy business of his own.

"Are you sure you know what he was doing over there?"

"I gotta believe my son."

Maggie understood that now no one would ever know what really happened, because the only witness to *whatever* Eddie Figueroa was doing where he was not supposed to be, Nelson Ashford, a thirty-six-year-old father, was conveniently dead. But, surprise! Someone else had lived to film the entire sordid undertaking.

"Who was that cameraman? What was *he* doing there?" Julio wanted to know.

The problem was that that night, Maggie was blasted. She had smoked crack and she felt like a ghost. She had been drinking out of a mini bottle, and she knew that Julio had to see it. It was the anxiety, it just never went away, she could not get the hunger under control that day. So she was agitated and fried, like fried *up*, and her heart was a broken piece of china watching Julio getting all worked up, crying and yelling. He never did that. Never. And Maggie wasn't together enough to talk him out of it. She just sat there. She could barely keep her head on her neck; the world was so heavy. So when Julio started cursing out the department and getting fiery . . .

"They aren't going to investigate," he insisted. "I know it. They are going to sell Eddie down the river because of Black Lives Matter and all those protestors the mayor wants to have as friends. I never saw a mayor who was so square and yet wanted to be so down-with-the-people as ours. He will let Eddie go *down*. I see it all happening, right before my eyes. He's a betrayer, that mayor. My wife, Maggie, you cannot imagine. The shame."

"I'm sorry."

"The thing is," Julio said. "Downtown, the brass. They want to find some Latino police officer to sacrifice, so they can say they were fair. Like that Asian cop in East New York who took the hit. You *never* see them prosecuting no white officers. Never. Then it's all *loyalty*. But when it is one of *us*! They will let Eddie go down like a sacrificial lamb."

And that's when the idea came up, and Maggie wasn't sure if she first suggested it, but someone suggested it and it had to be either her or Julio, but they somehow both came to believe that *they* would have to be the ones to investigate. That they knew what kinds of questions to ask, and they knew who to ask, and most importantly, they had those badges that let them ask.

Julio had the address of Martin Scott Bond, the guy with the camera phone. And Maggie felt . . . a thrill.

She felt some kind of grandiose rush, like *yeah, fuck,* she and Julio would show the department, and they would rescue Eddie, or at least get him a fair ride. That was all they wanted, for him to be treated fair. No one thought Ashford should have died, but why the fuck couldn't he just have cooperated? That's what they needed to ask Martin Scott Bond. And why was *he* there? They could blow this whole thing wide open. And she just needed to score a little coke, and then she would be gangbusters, literally. She and Julio agreed to go home after their shifts and eat a good dinner and then meet up later, badges in hand, at the address where Nelson was killed, where Eddie had taken a wrong turn, and go pay a visit to Martin Scott Bond, the fucker. Pay him a visit. The thing about everything is that there comes a point in life when a person can really understand why almost anything could happen.

But that was a long time ago. Now.

"Okay, Maggie?"

"Excuse me?"

Mike repeated himself. "Does that work for you, Maggie?"

"Can you just repeat the plan one more time?"

"Weird," Craig said to no one in particular.

"You will read through the files and send around a summary before you leave at the end of the day."

"Of course, Mike. No problem."

"Okay, everyone?"

"No problem."

CHAPTER SEVENTEEN

8:00 PM

Maggie stayed late at the office, as was expected. She read the files slowly, between cloudy dream times where the world seemed to leave her behind. Finally finished, she gently placed the folder in an empty file-cabinet drawer. If she could fulfill her responsibilities and keep this job, that cabinet might soon be full.

Sandy had given her a pen, and she placed it on the desk. Then she gathered her meager belongings and left the workroom, starting off for that other room called *home*. The journey down the elevator was rather unconscious and automatic, which seemed natural. Almost a normal response to a long day. But once out on the street, Maggie felt anxious again and could not imagine what would happen in that apartment *this* evening. She could see herself pacing and crying, and then what? So, she started wandering a bit. She started crossing streets without thinking, getting lost in the crowd. Maybe there would be someone to talk to. She checked the meeting list Rachel had prepared for her; there wasn't anything for an hour. She could get there twenty minutes early and set up chairs. But that still left forty dangerous minutes to kill, and so much could go wrong. She could wander and look in shopwindows. But disappearing into the world was even more alienating—and dangerous—than staying out of it.

Who were these people? They all seemed so happy. And rich. Where were the dark souls with their adventures and their wisdom that had made up the soil of this town? Gone? Were they dead? Everyone was well-dressed, everyone was somewhat ridiculous in their exhibition of expensive duplicates of each other's expensive things. The way people walked was different. What they discussed. They didn't emanate the big *we* that had brought her to this city in the first place. That instant sense of belonging that awaited all the sad and confused and angry types. Shoulder to shoulder, making their own choices toward every possible outcome. Talking. Bizarre. Together.

"From my Facebook feed, you would never know we're about to have a nuclear war with North Korea," said a young man to his date.

"Did you see my new phone? It's awesome."

The solitude was a shroud. It made her bones brittle and her joints rigid; it was disintegrating. The only thing the world offered her was a bottle of Miller High Life. And then a six-pack. And then a case. She kept walking.

Now Maggie was at Saint Luke's Church. A decision of some sort was in effect, but when had it taken place?

Sober Dance.

She stood out front for a few minutes. What were her options? She could go to a movie about nothing, be filled with pain, and then leave in the middle, sobbing, go to a restaurant and try to finish her meal, or cry alone at home.

Maggie wandered down a hallway, and again down those ever-present basement steps. AA was always in the basement, always in a crappy room, always on uncomfortable chairs. It had to be or it wouldn't feel right. It wouldn't work if it were formal. Or elegant. There had to be zero pretensions or no one would be able to show themselves, they would lie to impress, to compete with the carpet.

One of the guys at the rehab, Danny Bernstein, had been to a spa-like rehab for royalty in Malibu. They didn't have folding chairs, but in his case, it hadn't made a difference. The luxury did not make things take. So, he was back again with the rest of them, on those bad chairs. Maybe a person had to be uncomfortable to be uncomfortable, to realize they had to listen to other people's stories. That was the difference between the world and a meeting. Both could listen and hear without knowing, but knowing is what made it work. Keep coming back, even if you waste your time pretending because the next time you might actually learn something about how to be a person. Listening was not as implicating as most people imagined it to be. It actually saved lives.

Maggie peeked into the dance hall. Folks were having fun. Laughing. Used to being sober, or not. Some were dressed up, some were in work drag, some were just clean. It didn't matter how they looked; that wasn't important. What was important was to stay sober so that you could be authentic. The music was what it should be: in the middle and irrelevant. She looked around and finally recognized someone. Omar! From Saint Peter's basement. He was standing on the side, also looking around. He checked his watch. He was disappointed somehow. Then she saw him look up and see her, and burst into a big smile. Oh no, did he think this was a date? She knew it was the blond hair. Was that racist? Actually, it was. The only thing she had said in that meeting that morning was *scared*. Not really grounds for a friendship. Unless he was just being . . . egad . . . *nice*.

Suddenly, she fled.

It took an hour on the Q train to Brooklyn, and then a long walk from the station down Church to Caton and up Westminster toward an address she had long held memorized. It was the kind of neighborhood where inside and outside were parts of the same whole, and some of the apartment buildings, faded in their glory, still did not have functional locks on the front doors. Cars were public furniture, as people talked serious life business with neighbors in folding chairs. Still radios, some iPhones, but still some big old speakers. Bangladeshi families and Jamaican kids spilled out of hot apartments, sitting with plates of food. The sidewalk was the park, was the conference hall, the therapist's office, the employment center, the spiritual advisor, the banker, the predictor, the illusion, the dream. Maggie was out of place and she knew it. But she had come this far. When she'd first arrived in New York, she'd walk through someone else's neighborhood with respect and quiet caution. When she worked for the NYPD, she was always in street clothes, but her whiteness laid out a carpet of silence. Now, just a few years later, a white person in Brooklyn was a threat: of eviction, raised rents, irrelevant businesses, and disappearance. She carried the plague.

Maggie was going to fuck up tonight and that was the way it was. Doing the right thing was not going to happen, and the Next Best Thing was also out of the question. This would be dangerous, but better than a cocktail.

She walked past a fried-shrimp place, a liquor store, a boarded-up check-cashing place. There was a yuppie wine shop. Okay, these people were doomed. Whites move in latte first, and the wine shop follows. Next there would be organic food, then a bank. Maggie stopped outside a small private house. Terrified, she lifted the forbidden latch on the garden gate and walked onto the property, turning the house's corner, and looking in slyly, on the side of the structure. Breaking the law. There it was.

She looked through the window paralyzed with fear, and then with pain, because Maggie Terry, the reject of the world, stared at her *former* lover Frances, and her new . . . wife, *Maritza*, in their well-lit living room, where they were watching TV.

Frances had gained some weight. Her hair was long, longer than ever, but thin. Maritza was pretty, wearing a nightgown, sexy. Weirdly, as much as she spent her life thinking about Frances, it was always the *old* Frances. The *former* one. That's what happens when people refuse to talk; they get frozen in time. If Frances would just let them all be friends, things could catch up and they could remember what they loved about each other, and it could all become normal. Where was Alina? Would she come in at any moment? She was six now? Big and talkative in some new outfit? So far, far away. Who was she? If only Frances would let her know, let the longing be fulfilled. Frances had the power to do that. She was getting fat, that Frances. Probably still drinking. Please, Maggie was praying now. *Please.* She was trembling. It wasn't to God or the Higher Power, *as we understand Him*, it was to Frances. Because it was Frances who was actually in control.

Maggie had had this address for over a year. It was written on the documents, and she'd mapped it out plenty of times. But this, an actual in-person appearance, this was really crazy. And she knew it. For months she had been telling herself *don't contact Frances.* If she ever wanted to get Alina back, she had to follow the rules. But tonight, somehow the stakes were higher. If she didn't come and see it for herself, she was going to pick up. It was all that obvious. One connection or the other.

Maritza was not a high-risk girlfriend . . . uh . . . wife. She was not a player, just a nice woman, and a secretary at the Health Department and had ended up on Frances's floor. Everyone Maritza grew up with had a past, and as far as she was concerned, she lucked out big time with Frances. Frances could be the big one in this relationship, no danger of being overwhelmed by brains or looks or background or self-destruction. The two of them were watching a comedy of some kind. It looked boring. How could they do it? They were laughing, wearing slippers. TV was for people who came home, had dinner, watched a show, and then went to bed. Oh, now they were changing the channel. Rachel Maddow. Even Frances and Maritza were paying attention to politics now. Rachel looked like a swan. Wouldn't it be cool to be able to sit there with them on that nice couch? Maybe Alina could watch too. These people didn't have big things going on; they didn't have big things to avoid—or wait a minute, yes, they did. They had to collude on avoiding the pain they were causing Maggie. That was their conspiracy, the one that united them. That was their treaty, their pact. They were normal and if they kept Maggie away from Alina, then Alina would be normal, too. That was the phony deal.

They didn't have bad habits. They just wanted to snuggle on the couch: everything Maggie had never had, and didn't know how to have.

Was Alina reading in bed? Was she dreaming? Was she sassy? Was she nice?

Maggie tried to angle in closer, to check out the layout of the place, to see if she could get a glimpse of Alina's room. She was so close.

Frances stood up with an empty glass. She had gained a lot of weight, more than Maggie realized. She'd become one of those people who didn't care what she weighed. It was weird.

Frances picked up Maritza's teacup and started to the kitchen to get some refills. On the way, she turned to ask her wife something and then looked up, catching a figure in the window. Her hair was really gray. Frances didn't need to look good to keep Maritza. She was confident; she could let herself go.

Maritza was satisfied, and Maggie had never, ever

been satisfied. That was all Frances wanted. To be enough without having to try.

And then Maggie realized that Frances was looking right at her.

It was all so clear. She had wanted to get caught.

And now Frances had caught her.

Frances was staring, openmouthed. She was shocked.

Maggie felt great, even though she knew she was in trouble. She had made Frances look at her, see her. She had reminded Frances that the person she was tearing away from her own child was alive and real. *Success.*

Frances had thought she could have her way forever. That the status quo was eternal. Maggie saw, in her shock, that Frances had never imagined what Maggie imagined every day and every night: that Frances would eventually change her mind.

What was most important in Maggie's life was the least important consideration to Frances. Maggie had been waiting for Frances to see that she had been sober for eighteen months and two days. That she had a new job. That she was doing the work she was supposed to be doing.

But the reason Frances didn't realize this was that Frances had not done any work.

This was not acceptable to Maggie. The permanence of separation.

She had to make it plain that Frances was living a lie. The lie that she had nothing to be accountable for, and that only Maggie was wrong.

Frances said something to Maritza, who snapped

her neck and stared at Maggie with hate. Frances took out her phone and called the police, while Maritza lowered the drapes.

This option had not occurred to Maggie: calling the police and lowering the drapes. It was the wrong choice. The right choice was going outside, taking a walk together, and having a cup of coffee. How about some understanding? Some nuance? Some flexibility or rethinking? That is what she had expected, not more punishment. Not that.

Maggie hated Maritza. Lowering the blinds. What was that supposed to do? Pretend that things were not the way they are? It was cruel.

Maggie knew that the police would come. But she was stuck in her spot. Frances was still lazy. When would she do some labor so they could work something out? A child should know all her mothers.

Maggie heard a siren. So fast? Working people called the police more often than rich people. Poor people are used to the police in their lives. They had capitulated to the police as arbiters of their desperation, their relationships. The siren got closer. It probably wasn't for her. Why would there be a siren? But, then again, who knew what lie Frances had told the police? Maybe she told them Maggie had a gun.

Then Maggie ran. She knew that the police coming would be used as proof that nothing had changed, instead of the recognition that the status quo was unbearable.

Frances could have made things better, but she had decided to make things worse.

Maggie ran and then walked, as if not to be too suspicious, even though no one else looked like her. Wait, there were some gentrifiers; she could blend in. She slowed down even more, almost lackadaisical. Maggie knew it was possible she could be seized, and she made the decision to deny, and then cooperate. As a cop, it was better if someone stuck to their story. If they stuck with it, for years sometimes, sometimes they could get away with it. But she decided to try once, and then, if they brought Frances to ID her, she would just give in. She waited for the car's flashers to pull up beside her, as she approached the subway. Maybe they weren't looking for her yet. Maybe Frances was still filing the report.

Maggie almost tiptoed into the station. She was so careful now. She used her MetroCard, without a moment's hesitation. There was a waiting Q train; she stepped on it, and was gone.

Standing in the empty car, Maggie finally panicked. What had she done? Would they come after her? *Fluorescent.* A homeless man was sleeping. She looked at him, maybe it was someone she knew. She remembered Frances's happy family. Her lack of care. The homeless man was clutching a bottle of booze. Maggie reached for it. He moved. She saw her reflection in the subway window, superimposed on the passing neon BAR signs on the street and in her mind, the passing night, the hours, the lights of the city before her and below.

DAY THREE

FRIDAY, JULY 7, 2017

CHAPTER EIGHTEEN

7:00 AM

When she walked into Nick's she knew something was wrong. He was deep in conversation with Joe, who looked gray and shaken.

"Nick, are you okay?"

In the background the television was on, with thousands of German demonstrators throwing tear gas bombs back at the police. They had signs saying G-20 WELCOME TO HELL.

"Yeah, yeah." Nick waved his troubles away. "The usual?" He tried to find a smile as he made her mint tea and pulled out an unearthly green apple that was hard as a potato.

"You sure?"

Nick pointed to the freezer.

"What do you mean, Nick?"

He reached in, scooped up a cup of cubes. "ICE," he said.

"Oh, *immigration.*"

"They're taking people out," he mumbled. "All over the place."

The broadcast cut to Trump, himself, lips pursed in distaste, hair flapping.

"The fundamental question of our time is whether the West has the will to survive."

"I'm sorry, Joe."

"Okay." Joe was so pale. He disappeared into the dairy case.

Back at Saint Paul's, Joel M., who had seemed good-looking just the day before, was now sallow and clutching his stomach like he needed to puke, but couldn't let it happen. Martha L., on the other hand, seemed rested. Either she had done some yoga or someone was being very, very good to her. Or, maybe it was self-acceptance. Maggie looked at Martha's stand-out, sharp, corporate attire: lilac skirt suit, checked blouse, purple scarf. She looked fantastic. This woman could wear anything beautifully. Why was that? What did she have that made her so put-together, even when she was falling apart? Ramón was growing a mustache. He was envisioning something elaborate that would require upkeep—a hobby. Ronald had a copy of Rilke under his arm. Was it an assignment for class or did he really enjoy the poet of love? Alan walked in late. Charles looked *a lot* better today. Katrina was crying, sobbing through the meeting, but never raised her hand. She wasn't able to do service by sharing. Maggie felt a desire to help her out, but held back. Who was she to help anyone? There was Chris, a *newcomer*, at his first meeting. Yankel, an Orthodox Jew who had

had a slip and was back to counting days, instead of months. Suzanne, cringeworthy, another ubiquitous white woman in pain. Marva, a nurse in uniform, young thirties, filled with hope for a better life.

Maggie watched all these people going through their paces. It was her nature to keep track of them. She was observant, an information gatherer. The source of those compulsions was obvious: watching her parents crumple. Childhood was about watching helplessly as people fell apart and took their relationships with them. Her father was so unpredictable; she had had to keep a close eye on him. He'd be merry, then crazy, then angry, then gone. Her mother had seemed to literally fold before her eyes; her knees got weak and she fell inward, as Wolf, Maggie's father, lived up to his name. When her mother killed herself, there was a silence that Wolf filled with outbursts, grand gestures, big people, large feelings. Maggie's job was to keep track: Where were they going? Who was coming? What was the plan here? He'd promise big happiness: an *incredible* trip to the beach that would turn into a crashed car, a fight, a wrong turn and arriving four hours late. Maggie was a watcher, and she watched Wolf ruin everything. Then when he remarried Julie, he couldn't keep her drunk enough to hide that he was empty and mean. And one day she was gone, like a puppy who was given away. No goodbyes. Wolf had been impossible and Julie just left. Now Maggie missed Julie, and she had never even liked her. Was that how it worked? Each love holds the love before it? Maggie remembered holding Alina and reading her a book called *Everybody Poops*. Frances's mother had brought it over.

"Maggie loves Alina and Alina loves Maggie," Frances's mother said.

That was the greatest moment in Maggie's life. She was part of a family.

Other people, other people, other people, other people.

At 12 Step meetings there were so many different faces and personalities and stories, dreams, details, crises, episodes, frustrations, and expectations coming and going from those rooms. Strangely, for the first time in her life, Maggie felt that she did not want to know *everything* that was going on. It would have been impossible anyway, unless she'd worn a wire and recorded it all for her files. She had to give up her impulse to try to understand what was happening with every single other person. This meeting was the one family that Maggie didn't have to maneuver to hold on to. It was always there for her. She didn't need an invitation, and she couldn't be excommunicated. She just had to show up.

"My husband . . ."

She listened, but tried to not remember the person's name. She didn't want *friends*; she couldn't handle the responsibility right now. Should she raise her hand and share?

Telling the story of what had happened the night before would take longer than the allotted three minutes. Was that always going to be the case? Keep It Simple. It seemed that most shares had to do with going to work, looking for work, the ever-increasing stress of Trump destroying the nation, and, always, relationships. Most shares did not involve strangled actresses and jumping on trains to avoid the police, but some did. Overall, it was banality that was the bond, and having a story that was too big would break that bond. She needed to not stand out. It would be good for her. Stay sober! Whatever she had to do to not pick up, that was what she should do.

She raised her hand. Someone else was called on. Ronald.

Maggie was kind of relieved, kind of pissed off. As Ronald started describing his obstacle, trying to lay out his choices, Maggie practiced what she was going to share. She ran it through in her mind to get the share down to three minutes. So, I went to see my daughter to negotiate with her mother to create a humane . . .

"I just ask my Higher Power," Ronald was saying, "to help me, help me understand. Because I can't figure it out on my own."

Everyone clapped.

Maggie was thinking so hard, she forgot to raise her hand again. Ramón got called on. *Higher Power* meant that they all needed some mercy, some exterior kindness, someone else wanting to make things right. Right? But Frances wasn't sitting in a meeting trying to deal with her actions. She was watching TV with her arm around her new wife, thinking that meant she had won. It was so strange. Maggie seemed to be the only person in this cast of characters who was actually trying to deal with everything. And for there to be a solution, they both had to be doing it, Maggie and Frances. Technically, Frances qualified for Al-Anon, and frankly also for AA. How could Maggie get Frances to recognize this and go to meetings too so that they could start talking about what really mattered? Getting visitation with Alina.

Ramón was describing the experience of trying to save up for a car, and how it was a symbol, concrete evidence of making something out of his life. Did Maggie need a car? No, she remembered. She needed curtains and a tea bag.

"First Things First," said Ramón.

First Things First.

She raised her hand.

"Hi, thanks for calling on me. My name is Maggie and I am an alcoholic and a drug addict."

"Hi, Maggie."

Omar walked in.

"I feel like . . . like . . . I'm *supposed* to . . . acknowledge all the 'destruction' . . . I've . . . 'caused.' But I don't want to. I don't feel like it's all my fault. I *feel* like . . . it just happened. And I want to know . . . why is this my life? Thank you."

That wasn't what she had meant to share. She had meant to share the pain of Frances making the wrong decision. The decision that served no one but Frances's need to feel superior. Maggie was so frustrated that she hadn't said what she needed to say that she forgot again to call on the next person. Then the pressure of all the staring, hungry eyes finally bore through her thick skull.

"Sorry."

She pointed to Omar.

"Thanks for calling on me. My name is Omar; I am a drug addict."

She did not want to hear what Omar had to say. She

did not want to get to know him. She did not want to get involved with all these people who were dangerous to themselves, whom she could hurt. And then, some terrible pain exploded inside. Missing Frances. Regret. Where was her beautiful child? Why didn't anyone love Maggie Terry?

"Thank you." Omar was done. He smiled at her and called on Charles.

Maggie felt terrible that she hadn't listened. What had this man done to her besides being welcoming and kind? She had n-o-t-h-i-n-g but her sobriety. Who was she to be a snob? Was that what she was? A bitch? Really? Let's get honest.

They all stood for the Serenity Prayer.

Maggie again left out the word *God*. But this time she did stay for the entire closing. *Changing the things I can.* Honestly, that was almost anything, but not everything. She couldn't *change* a court order, but she could get it reversed. Anything a human being created, a human being could change.

And the wisdom to know the difference.

The meeting was over and Maggie beelined for Omar.

"Omar, I apologize for my behavior at the dance."

"Thank you so much, Maggie. It's your right to decide whether or not you want to be at a dance."

"True."

"At least you checked it out."

The Next Best Thing.

"But it's not my right to be rude to you."

He smiled a huge, truly happy smile of reward, surprise, and contentment. "That is a wonderful gift.

Thank you so much." Then he handed over his card. "Here is my phone number. If you ever want to get together over coffee . . ."

That was the problem with taking responsibility, Maggie remembered. Everything becomes deeper. It is not a way out of life, it is only a way in.

"After what I just shared? Omar, what in the world would make you want to get together with me?"

"You are honest about how defensive you are. But still think you are a special case. Maggie, you are not the most fucked-up person in the room. No one is. You are competing for a position that doesn't exist. Everyone needs support."

He smiled, but in a gentler way. She was suspicious. What did he want?

"I have to get to work."

Maggie picked up her uneaten apple and her cold cup of mint tea and walked to the office, placing the apple in her shoulder bag with today's newspaper, where it knocked against the apple left over from the day before. Maybe she didn't like apples. How could that be? Maybe she should stop buying them at Nick's until she found something she actually wanted? What would she eat? A bagel? The thought seemed repulsive.

"Good morning, Maggie," Sandy warmly greeted her at reception. "How are you today?"

"Okay," Maggie mumbled, distracted. She started stumbling toward her personal version of an empty refrigerator, i.e., her office, when suddenly she turned around. "Sandy?"

"Yes?"

"How are you?"

"I'm excited, actually."

"Why?"

There it was again. Other people.

"Because," and Sandy actually jumped up and down and clapped her hands like a TV nursery school teacher in 1964, "I have some great news for you."

"For me?"

"Yes, Maggie, your office is finally ready!" And Sandy grabbed her hand and led her down the hallway. "Look!"

On the gray door was stenciled: MS. MAGGIE TERRY, PRIVATE INVESTIGATOR.

"Isn't that cool?"

"Yeah," Maggie said, realizing that someone was telling her that she was going to be there for a while. That she was welcomed. "Mike is such a doll."

"Actually, I did it," Sandy reported calmly, and burst into giggles. "But Mike approved it, of course."

Maggie opened the door, hoping that someone else had taken care of everything; maybe Sandy was the new daddy, the new *good* daddy, and Maggie would no longer have to do the hard work of *decorating* when she didn't know what she liked. But, of course, the room was still empty. *Shit!* She had forgotten to pick up curtains and tea bags for her apartment again. She *had* to do it. Maybe during lunch? Then, she had a better idea. The right idea. Maggie stood in the doorway, reached into her bag, pulled out the green orb and the mealy red one, and finally bit into each apple. Then she drank the cold tea. First Things First. Then she took out her cell phone and dialed one of the two numbers in her contacts.

"Hi, it's Maggie. Can we meet for lunch?"

"Sure, did you watch Rachel Maddow last night? The Trump people are sending forged NSA documents to the media, trying to trick them into printing fake stories, so they can accuse the media of being fake."

"No, I don't have a TV." Everyone she met was talking about the world. Maggie could never remember a society so united by threats regularly announced on television.

"You can watch it online. Okay, come by the office. See you soon. First Things First."

CHAPTER NINETEEN

1:00 PM

The droning of the drill made Maggie's teeth hurt. That was the one thing about Rachel she had never understood: not her tales of incessant and insane cocaine use that were, *today*, invisible and unimaginable. Not her difficult journey toward transsexuality, as Maggie had always known her as the woman she is. Not her fanatically left-wing politics that made her sponsoring a former police detective a state of contradiction, not Rachel's constant embrace of contradiction, but *how in the hell* could Rachel spend most of her life with her hands in other people's mouths?

The waiting room was like any dentist's office: pastel, demure on the edge of boring, but the magazine rack held the *Nation*, the *Guardian*, and printouts of each morning's edition of the *Electronic Intifada*. *Democracy Now!* played on the sound system. The reporter, Amy Goodman, had the most no-nonsense voice

Maggie had ever heard. She was saying something about Raqqa being "slaughtered silently." What, Maggie wondered, was Raqqa?

A thin, macraméd curtain separated the waiting patients from those in the dentist's chair, and Maggie could hear all of the banter.

"Now, rinse."

Or,

"Every day there is a new impeachable offense. When are the Republicans going to stop using him to get richer, and help the Democrats kick him out on his ass?"

Or,

"I can't do anything if you won't floss your teeth. We have to work together to keep you chewing."

Even dentists were fluctuating between panicking about the government and the coercions of daily existence.

Soon Rachel emerged in her sleeveless red linen tunic from Eileen Fisher, plaid cotton skirt from Ann Taylor, and black Birkenstocks. "I'm on my feet all day, you know." And they headed down the block for lunch.

Veselka had been on the corner of Ninth Street and Second Avenue since before Rachel was born, and she had been eating there all of her life. In homage to that life, she usually ordered the cold borscht with homemade challah bread and a cherry lime rickey. Since Maggie only ever came to this place with her sponsor, Rachel usually encouraged her to dip into the depths of Ukrainian delights. But to Maggie, it all looked unappetizing. Sour cream might be too sour. *Kasha varnishkes*, butterfly pasta covered in thick mushroom gravy, seemed like wallpaper paste; and the stuffed cabbage being devoured at the next table appeared to be some kind of stringy substance wrapped around an advanced Eastern European meatball. So while Rachel gobbled her side of potato pancakes, a half order of fried pierogi, and a side of kielbasa with gusto and glee, Maggie ordered a BLT on whole-wheat toast that she could have had anywhere in the United States. She just could not assimilate one new thing. *Today.*

If Rachel was disappointed in Maggie's rejection of new experiences, she kept it to herself. This relationship, after all, was not about her. It was about keeping Maggie sober, and in order to stay sober Maggie had to address her anxieties. To do that, she had to work the steps, go to meetings, and talk to her sponsor. The fact that Maggie had called meant that she had *asked for help*, and that was a move in the right direction. For this reason, Rachel was there to listen and advise, just as Rachel's original sponsor, Matias, may he rest in peace, had listened so closely so many years before.

Maggie slowly recounted her maladjustment at work, the pressure of Craig's disapproval, Brinkley's pass and subsequent tailing, the command of drugs and alcohol from every corner. The loneliness. The paltry service at meetings. Her dismissal of Omar, her ambivalences about her own actions. Enid's active hatred of her. Sandy's kindness. And her ongoing inability to get her apartment organized. She entirely omitted any information about having taken the train to Frances's house and Frances calling (or perhaps pretending to call) the police, since no one had contacted her with any warnings, legal or otherwise. Every time it came to a place in the conversation where she could have brought that up, it seemed less grave. She focused her story down to the struggle to stay away from substances.

"I bring you check," said the Ukrainian waitress, wearing a small blue-and-yellow flag pinned to her apron.

"*Dziękuję*," Rachel responded with enthusiasm, as it was her habit to try to speak to people in their own languages to whatever degree possible. "I think that might be Polish," she confided as the waitress picked up their cash.

"And how are *you*?" Maggie finally asked as they walked out past the Rice Krispies treats and black-and-white cookies at the front counter by the door.

"Danny and I are having a big party for our nineteenth anniversary. I want you to be there."

"Thank you so much."

"And then we're going to Hawaii."

"Nineteen years of happiness." Maggie felt hopeless. "I admire you so much."

"Well, it came after ten years of sobriety."

"I'm forty-two." She had eighteen months and three days. She would be fifty-one when she had ten years. If she met someone then, if they could last nineteen years, she would be seventy.

"Fifty-two is not too old to meet the love of your life," Rachel said with gravitas. She meant it. "Also sixty-two."

"That does give me some time to decorate my apartment."

They walked up Second Avenue to Rachel's office.

184

"Maggie, listen to me. I have many sober years, but each one starts with One Day at a Time. Tonight, on your way home from work, buy a bunch of flowers for your apartment and a vase to put them in. That will start you creating a foundation for building a home where you will love to be. A safe haven. The first step of many steps."

"Okay." Maggie looked at her watch. "I want to."

"Good. What is next for you, *today?*"

"I have to get back to the sexually abusive father of a murdered mentally ill young actress."

Rachel seemed, well, concerned. "Why?"

"It's my job."

She laughed. "Put that on your list of things to think about."

"Okay, Doctor Rachel. Wish me luck."

"Where is he living?"

"In a slum apartment."

"Is it owned by Jared Kushner? He owns that one." She pointed across the street. "And that one."

"I don't know."

"Maggie," Rachel wrapped her arms around her, "I believe in you. Buy flowers!"

Walking east and south to Stefan Wagner's building, it was hard to believe how much this area of the city had changed. There was a Starbucks on Saint Mark's Place and Avenue A. There were new luxury constructions everywhere, with placards advertising "One bedrooms starting at 1.6 million." There were buildings with pools on the roof, and movie stars buying entire buildings and adding floors they didn't need just to show off their wealth to the squeezed, rent-stabilized tenants next door. Every so often there was still some eccentric low-cost variety: a Vietnamese sandwich stand, a walk-in that only sold pork sandwiches to go, a little shed with a guy shaving ice off a large slab and adding plum juice. Some old bars. This went on and on: bad expensive restaurants, bars selling food that only belonged in the suburbs, with undesirable themes like German sausage haus. On corners where Maggie had once bought dope in peace, there were ubiquitous $5 doughnut shops. Everything that should cost a dollar now cost five. And boring people, looking the same, same, same, until suddenly, it was a strip that hadn't yet been seized. There were still some auto parts stores. There was a Chinese bridal shop. Some storefront churches stayed strong between the last of the bodegas with plantains and yucca in the window. There were unrenovated businesses, some old men sitting on a stoop, and garbage. Where did they go to buy food? How did they get secondhand refrigerators? Where did they get their shoes repaired? Oh, there was a shoe repair! Lots of garbage. The garbage cans were chained, but not sealed, so the place had rats.

But when she got to Stefan's building, one of the few dirty tenements still on the block, it was clear from who came running down the stairs and out the front door that these new tenants were paying $4,000 a month, and their apartments were probably newly constructed palaces, hiding behind the crumbling facade. They didn't look her in the eye, and she was white. But those $4,000-types would rather have rats than meet their neighbors. It would never occur to them that if they called a meeting, they could get the landlord to deal with the garbage, because these kinds of people *identified* with the landlord. So, they never complained. It was the passive mentality of the over-privileged. *Someone else* should take care of it. Maggie knew from her days driving to crime scenes with Julio, that—even with gentrification—there were still people in these buildings who had been there forever. Some of them wished they still had a neighborhood. But some of them just wanted to be left alone.

She pressed buzzer 5F, no name. No answer. So she waited.

Finally, a white guy with a thick neck and a coordinated running outfit came out the door, earbuds already in place. He didn't look her in the eye, so he didn't notice her foot in the closing door as she let herself into his hallway. These kids had zero street smarts. It would be so easy to rip them off.

The hallways had been renovated and the gentrified apartments had new doors. She could see that there were only a few of the original tenants left, waiting to drop like flies. But the rickety stairs still had burn marks sealed into the slate. A lot of junkies died in this building, she thought, as there was no sign of them beyond the cigarette scars they'd left behind on the steps. The oral history passed down by drug addicts told of days before Maggie's time. The ghosts of young men yelling *Ba Hondo!* when the cops were coming, and gasoline envelopes with hand rubber stamps advertising Toilet-brand heroin, or Watergate. There were no monuments to the thin Puerto Rican women whose lives were lost waiting on line to buy dope out of buckets lowered from abandoned buildings, where blue glass towers now stood guarded by doormen, and featuring four-star restaurants. No plaques saying "A person in this building died of AIDS." No sign. No sign. It never happened at all. Pretend, pretend, pretend. Like Frances, refuse history.

Apartment 5F was not hard to find. Old chipped red paint, three locks, and a warped tilt indicated the cave of Jamie Wagner's father. It was also the one blasting classical music, the kind she grew up on. The only thing Maggie and Wolf could do in the same room. Of course, lots of different kinds of people listened to classical music, but they would be more likely to have a better sound system than the tenant in 5F. It was so staticky it seemed to be coming from . . . a radio, not even a computer. She knew she had her man. Maggie knocked.

No answer.

"Mister Wagner?" she called out. "Mister Wagner?"

The scratchy notes continued.

"Mister Wagner, it's Maggie Terry, the investigator. We have an appointment to talk about your child."

CHAPTER TWENTY

2:30 PM

Slowly, very slowly, the door crept open at the hands of a defeated, exhausted old fellow. He was sad. His apartment was sad; his life was sad and things had been that way for a very, very long time. They would never be fixed. And that had apparently been true even before his fetishized daughter's promising, wounded life had come to a terrible, sudden, and violent close.

Stefan Wagner smelled. He was rotting, and he didn't care. He was the kind of man tired people would stand on the subway to avoid sitting beside. He was angry and scared and entirely unreliable. His suit was lived in; his shirt was yellowed. His life was one of misery, with a single, sterling exception . . . his beautiful and successful daughter, Jamie. No wonder he had wanted so badly to be near her.

"I don't like bureaucrats, doctors, government officials," he said.

"Good, because I am none of the above. Is that Mendelssohn?"

"Yes."

Was there ever a day that Maggie's class and education did not come in handy? What did people do who had not grown up going to the symphony? She'd escaped marrying a boy like her father, or even a boy the opposite of her father, rejected being a lady who lunched, refused the garden club, and said NO to taking the commuter train into the city from some suburban hell to see a matinee as a way of life. She had become a professional in a man's field, and she had learned a lot about how people really lived. Sometimes she learned the hard way, but Maggie had accrued a lot of information. A lot. Not enough, but a lot. She wasn't afraid of lost, confused souls like Stefan Wagner; she was used to them. She was at home with people who no one else could handle. The shitty apartments, the crazed manias.

It was all coming back to her. This was the world she had lived in every day. This was the world she and Julio had shared. The topsy-turvyness of the whole thing, the otherworldliness. That lack of rules was really what let her and Julio agree that they needed to make that godforsaken plan. To meet in the Bronx and *talk* to Martin Scott Bond. Both she and Julio knew that was a euphemism, they didn't say it to each other, but at that point, with Maggie high all the time and Julio crazed with worry about his son's life, they both *knew* that what they really were going to do was . . . well, to put it honestly, they were going to break the law they had both promised to uphold. They were intending to show up at Martin Scott Bond's crappy apartment and . . . *intimidate* him . . . into . . . withholding evidence . . . because . . . because, well, as Julio said, "The department is not protecting Eddie, and that is what they are supposed to be doing. And you know, Maggie, it's because he's Latino and they need to find a cop to make an *example* of, and that's not gonna be no white cop. And I can't let them destroy my son's life for doing what any of them and their fathers and sons would do—shoot to kill if you don't know what's what—but we have to protect our own."

"Yeah, Julio, yeah." Maggie was at triple speed. "Yeah, yeah, yeah, yeah, yeah." And who knows how far they would have gone, what they ultimately would have done to poor Martin Scott Bond, who was presenting himself as an innocent bystander.

"How come he was there?" Julio was sweating, shaking. "He was *implicated*, and he's blaming it on my son, with that motherfucking footage!"

Maggie was just supposed to "eat dinner," which meant do some coke, and change her clothes and meet Julio at Bond's apartment at nine, but how was she supposed to know that that was the night, *that very night* that Frances—goddamn her—Frances had arranged for an intervention.

Julio was sitting in his car, fuming and out of his mind, waiting for his partner of eleven years to come be by his side as they both broke the selectively applied modern law of regulations, and instead carried out the ancient law of tribe, where a man defended his son no matter what. As he was waiting for her, and as she, having done two lines at Georgie's, intended to get back up there, Frances was also waiting, but she was prepared.

"If you fight this, Maggie, you will NEVER see Alina again. I promise you. I will get you a narcotics arrest and that will be the end of your life. You will never be a cop again, you will never see me again, and you will never ever see your daughter again, as long as I live, unless you go to detox right now!"

What could she do?

The joke was—and Maggie was laughing even today, eighteen months and three days later, standing in a firetrap with a sick old man, listening to Mendelssohn—the joke was that Frances was lying. Frances was already involved with Maritza and she wanted Maggie out of the picture. Frances had no intention of ever sharing custody, and Frances didn't give a fuck about Maggie's career. But Maggie was too stoned to notice what a liar Frances had become. How cold. Foolishly believing that there was actually a choice being offered between Alina, on one hand, and Julio's love for Eddie, on the other, Maggie chose Alina without hesitation. And she felt good about that choice. In fact, she felt relieved. This would be it. Her moment of goodness had finally dawned.

So, she said yes to giving up everything and being dragged off to a hospitalization that only Frances could pull her out of. Finally, Maggie Terry would do something right. She would tell the truth. She would submit. She would be a team player, and then everyone could live together forever, happily ever after because Frances had finally shown, for real, that she cared. This was Frances's way of making Maggie's dream come true. Frances was saying, "I will work with you." She was saying, "We will do this together." She was saying, "I am here."

So, Maggie sat and waited for the EMT. Sitting very still, knowing that happiness was finally in front of her, all because someone else in her life finally came through—finally, did not disappear.

Only, it didn't work out that way.

In reality, Maggie never saw Julio again. Maggie never worked as a police detective again, and she never got high again. And she never saw her child again. Never. And here she was. Frances had lied.

Wasn't it weird, how much Maggie had trusted her? She must have loved her.

"Do you like Mendelssohn, Miss Terry?" Stefan Wagner slowly reached toward his wobbly cassette player and raised the volume. He could not hear the static. He could not hear the chaos of the lag in the tape's loop. He smiled.

"It's gorgeous." Maggie pulled a professional facade out of the grab bag of her past. "Mendelssohn used this sonata form for his *Hebrides* overture, I believe. Isn't that right Mr. Wagner?"

"Exactly." He had an accent as thick as Colonel Klink in *Hogan's Heroes*.

"But why?"

He returned to his clearly habitual seat on his newspaper-covered bed, leaving her a book-filled chair to negotiate. "Because it has a fairly strict pattern to follow, in form, as well as key and temperament."

She could see now that it wasn't a radio at all, but a decades-old rickety cassette player, in this shabby, grim life.

"I see, can I move these?"

"Let me." He carefully lifted one of the piles and placed it on the floor, leaving her a side of the chair to share with the other two stacks.

"Thank you."

He was reassured now. It was all going to be fine. "Most authorities don't know anything about music."

"I am a private citizen," Maggie said calmly. "I was once a government employee, but I had some emotional problems and now I am a private detective working for a law firm. No government."

He nodded. Stefan Wagner would love AA. He very much wanted to identify. "Yes, people are very cruel when you become upset. They don't allow for it." He crossed his legs, no socks on under a disastrous pair of shoes.

"Do you think, Mr. Wagner, that Jamie also had some emotional problems?"

"She was so beautiful." And then he started to cry.

As Maggie watched him weep she saw that he was a person who had never stopped crying. That when she knocked on his door he had been crying.

"If she wasn't my daughter I would have married her."

Check. Just as Steven had reported.

"I see."

"I'm sorry, I didn't offer you a drink; I never have company."

Maggie was still taken aback by the casual confession of his previous comment. That was not the kind of thing one says to a private investigator unless it was thought perfectly normal to have wanted to marry one's murdered daughter.

With great effort, Stefan slowly got down on his knees and reached under the bed. He wanted to do this, so she didn't stop him. Some groaning and mispositioning finally produced a dusty, clear bottle. He sat back down, dustballs on his pants legs, filthy bottle in his lap.

"Kirschwasser."

"No, thank you."

"Just a little. It is an old German liqueur."

"I don't drink."

He poured a shot into an old coffee cup sitting by his bed and then left it untouched.

"I am sadder than sad." His shoulders were slumped, lost in that horrible suit, a wreck of a life without its last oar. "Jamie and I shared so much in common."

"Like what?"

"Neither of us could sleep. We used to talk to each other on the phone at four in the morning. She would call me, or I would call her. We were free in that way, to be sure the other had company when it was necessary. Maybe now I will throw away my telephone." He indicated a dust-covered dial phone with a cracked black plastic receiver.

The rickety cassette tape kept turning in the player, a bit slack in parts. The music was an eerie ghost of greatness past, while the machine itself remained a stark document to decline and how it becomes inevitable. Most people in that building probably didn't know what a cassette was.

"Stefan, can you tell me about the last time you saw your daughter?"

She was listening very closely. There were some children outside. They must be the kids of the final Dominicans on the block. White yuppie children don't play on the streets. They are controlled. These kids spoke English with those disappearing New York accents, the friendly way of talking. It was so casual, it made friends just by hanging out in the air like a handshake. Never shy, it too was being replaced by Valley Girl uptones and Midwestern drones. She heard the pigeons cooing. This apartment, this moment, these sounds. They were all the past. It was floating so far away. People like Stefan couldn't get a lease anymore. They ended up homeless.

"I tried to call her many times. She is the only one I call." He looked again, mournfully, at the useless phone, a coffin of itself. "I called and called but she wouldn't speak to me. Then finally she answered and screamed in my ear."

"What did she say?"

"*You're sick*, she said." He was so shaken. Her anger survived the grave. "*I'm calling the police.*" He looked down at his hands, a fresh wound on top of ancient fresh wounds, each infecting the one before so that nothing ever heals. "Maggie, you are the police . . ."

"Not anymore."

"Why does everyone threaten to call the police? It

never helps anybody. Why punish all the time? Why not accept and let us live together?"

"Did she call the police?"

"No."

"Do you think you're sick?" Maggie asked.

"Yes."

"And you made Jamie sick?"

"No, it was that man. The boyfriend."

You're sick. Maggie had said that herself. It must be something that sick people say.

Frances said it too. That night. That night that it all came to an end.

Maggie looked at Stefan Wagner. She waited. Tried again, "Did your daughter Jamie ever actually call the police on you?"

"No, she never did." Stefan threw his hands up in the air, an old European gesture. "Finally I waited for her by the stage door."

"And then what happened?"

He described standing outside, on a cold windy spring evening filled with joy that he would soon see his beloved daughter.

Maggie sat still as he told her his story. She didn't want to remind him that she was there so he could feel alone, feel comfortable. She didn't cough or cross her legs. She was like the breeze.

It all unfolded clearly, carefully. Jamie's play had ended and the fans were gathering around the stage door to get the stars to sign their programs. His daughter played the housemaid hired by wealthy aristocrats in their country estate. Jamie brought the coffee tray onstage and then, later in the play, she came back, picked it up, and took it offstage. She had two lines:

"Coffee, mum?" She was directed to say it in a Cockney accent to vaguely indicate Britain's class system, and to add a bit of the saucy.

And the inevitable "Will that be all, then?" inserted by a playwright who clearly had no imagination.

Jaime had done hours of research to create backstory for her character. She gave her a name, Nancy, even though the program just said Housemaid. She gave her sex with a chauffeur to get off of her father's farm, then a love affair with the son of an archduke, and a stint as a prostitute in London's underworld. She gave her an interest in tarot cards, theosophy, Madame Blavatsky, and the occult. And a habit of padding her worn serving shoes with a piece of ribbon to give her aching feet a rest.

"How do you know all these details?" Maggie asked.

"We told each other everything. Even our sexual fantasies."

"At four in the morning when she couldn't sleep."

"That's right. We gave each other comfort."

Which he clearly thought was a good thing. The "comfort" that caused pain in all of her relationships.

"In her first scene . . ." Stefan was enjoying the telling now. "After saying her line 'Coffee, mum?' There was a twenty-eight-minute monologue about being a queen who was dethroned, while Jamie, as Nancy, listened."

"For twenty-eight minutes."

"Listening actively is a difficult skill onstage. Jamie trained for this by watching performances of O'Neill plays like *The Iceman Cometh* and *A Moon for the Misbegotten*, where actors had to actively listen for very long periods of time. She also studied the play *Balm in Gilead* by Lanford Wilson, in which an actress named Glenne Headly had a monologue long enough for every person in the theater to work through a personal problem they had been putting off indefinitely. Every night, Lucy's monologue ended in applause. And when the adulation finally died down, Jamie a.k.a. Nancy a.k.a. Housemaid would pick up the tray and say, 'Will that be all, then?'"

Maggie saw something she hadn't expected to see. She saw that for all the dysfunction that really was abuse, and actually was criminal; that simultaneous to this terrible use of his child, he loved her. Who else was out there reveling in her performance of "Coffee, mum?" Not Steven Brinkley. He was waiting for bigger things. And this new understanding helped Maggie see Jamie Wagner in a more positive light. For despite the inescapable destruction of her boundaryless, dangerous father, Jamie wanted to make every second of her tiny life-in-progress count for something. For the first time, Maggie had a glimpse of what Steven Brinkley had seen and then committed to: Jamie was really an artist. She had drive and intelligence. When it came to acting, she made the best of it, despite all the obstacles within and without her, and her terrible loyalty to a father who was her biggest problem, and the sad way she blamed Steven Brinkley for pain he had not caused.

In other words, aside from being murdered, Jamie had everything that Maggie wanted. She was loved. She had a future. And she was forgiven.

"So what happened when she stepped out of the theater that night and saw that you were waiting for her? Even after she had yelled at you on the phone?"

Like he'd said, it was a cold, windy spring evening. Stefan had stayed back from the crowd of hungry fans and watched until his daughter emerged, unnoticed, slipping past the principle actors and down the stairs to unlock her bicycle, which was chained to a No Parking sign against the curb. He'd walked up to her, bereft.

"I'd said, 'Jamie,' And then she started screaming. On the street. Like a mad person."

"What did she say?"

"She said . . ." He paused with the pain of it all, all the pain that had become his life now that he was here and his child was not. "She said, 'Get away, I told you to leave me alone.'"

"What did you do?"

"I said, 'It's that man. Your boyfriend. He's ruined everything between us, can't you see that?'"

Stefan was crying again now. That was the second man Maggie had seen weep openly because of Jamie's accusations, even more so than her death.

"Then she said, 'He's sick, too. All my men are sick. I have to get away from all of you. I have to find someone who doesn't want anything from me, who doesn't need anything, who has no opinions. And I will find them, I will.' And with that she jumped on her bike."

Maggie processed his story. Jamie had two loves in her life. One, her father, was destructive and distorting. She would have had to fully face his betrayal to allow the other, Steven, who really saw her, to help her heal. But she got confused. She could not tell them apart.

"And then?"

"That was it." Stefan's tears would never stop. "The last thing I saw was the flip of her hair and then—my beautiful Jamie—she was gone."

Stefan is a liar, Maggie suddenly understood. And the lie is that he was clean. The lie is . . . that he . . . loved his child.

If Maggie wanted her own life to make sense, she would have to brush away that same lie of innocence. *Whoosh.*

And at that moment, she realized something much worse—that maybe Alina was better off without her, without knowing that she was missing. Not whimpering, afraid, not confused, not living with unpredictability, but fine. Absolutely fine with her mom and her new mommy, what's-her-name, and content and quiet and fingering her own newly clean ears after a bath that someone else had given her. Whatever tiny piece of her heart Maggie Terry could still access while in professional drag got used for showing up to work and showing up to meetings, and basically not much more. Then, that morsel of life that was Alina had to stay deeply buried in her soul, so low it was in her ankle somewhere, that little crumb of feeling.

CHAPTER TWENTY-ONE

6:30 PM

It was early evening. Maggie stepped out of the subway station, exhausted again. It was all too much. There were so many vortexes of struggle and defeat as the pain of the community around Jamie Wagner's corpse converged with the absence circling Maggie's dead life.

She was about to turn down her street when, suddenly, she actually remembered she had to buy tea bags. That was a sign of progress, after all. Every minute was so up and down. Now where should she get them? Maggie noticed the first store in her path was the gourmet snack shop Nick had complained about. What were its treasures laid out before her? Was this the Higher Power she could sign up for? The right store at exactly the moment that she remembered what she was supposed to do. Now, maybe that was the "God" they were all bragging about. Just doing what a person was supposed to do.

Their tea selection was overwhelmed by extravagant flavors like Afghani spirit, named for the people that the United States just could not stop murdering. Smoky sesame lime, the sum total of a flavor combination that provided no clue to actual taste. Promises of spiritual expansion were offered by soul-widening tea, and then, of course, she could select something that offered escape from having to think or feel: doze tea, meditation green, and sleep tea. She finally bought California peppermint because it was the closest to the generic mint that Deli Nick had gotten her drinking in the mornings.

Okay, mission accomplished!

Should she get anything else? What about breakfast? Yogurt? That sounded healthy. She looked at the dairy case: Greek yogurt, Bulgarian yogurt, goat milk yogurt, sheep milk yogurt, almond milk yogurt, tofu yogurt, coconut milk yogurt, and soygurt. She bought Greek and a banana to cut into it. And then she realized that she needed a knife.

"Do you have a knife?"

"I can give you a plastic one."

"Okay, thanks." And . . . carefully and cautiously, she picked up a *New York Times*, scanned the front page. It was very dense and filled with frightening events presented in a casual way, with hysterical undertones, and some sarcasm: "Trump and Putin: Where the Mutual Admiration Began," "Carl Reiner: Justice Kennedy, Don't Retire," "As Elites Switch to Texting, Watchdogs Fear Loss of Transparency." The stories were so complicated now that it was hard to find headlines to sum them up. The reader had to already know what was going on.

"Uhhh, can you throw in a late-edition *New York Post*, please?"

Something was missing. Oh yeah, *flowers*. She looked around, there was a man across the street selling them from the front of his shop.

Maggie paid for her shopping and crossed the avenue, floating directly into the arms of the gorgeous white roses calling out, heads opened and welcoming, and took them to her chest where she buried her face in their goodness. They were so soft. Yes, Rachel was right again, this was what she needed more of in her life.

"Hey you," a gruff voice called out. "Get away from those flowers. Buy first, then touch."

"FUCK OFF, asshole." Maggie was shocked by her own rage. "Don't yell at me." It wasn't the best choice of all the available responses, but he was killing her buzz. The happy-to-be-making-progress vibe was finally just starting to creep into her heart and this jack-off was ruining it.

"Don't tell me what to do." The guy was not having it. He was mad at the myriad of burdens propelling him, and he just didn't want another one. "You'd better buy something or I'm calling the cops."

Everyone is calling the cops. That's all people do in this city: threaten to call the police or call the police. How about a little conversation?

"I am a cop," Maggie lied.

"Oh yeah?" He doubted her but wasn't completely sure. "Where is your badge?"

"I was a cop. I got kicked out for alcoholism and drug addiction."

"Well," he said, confused. A tinge of empathy, of

identification, of objectification, of disdain. "You'd better buy something—one, two, three."

Thirty minutes later, safely at home, she stood in the doorway of her apartment, hands behind her back as though in handcuffs. And then—*one, two, three*—she brought them around to her front and presented herself with a present that no one else could have given her. She had to give it to herself . . . a plant! In fact, a cactus. Something autobiographical. If she forgot to water it for a month, it would still live. Maggie held it forth as an offering to her empty room.

"For me."

Now, where to place it?

She tried out the windowsill, but it was a bit too narrow and it would be depressing to come home to a fallen cactus.

She sat it in the middle of the floor, like a beacon under the bar light bulb. And then Maggie realized that someone was actually calling her landline. It must have been repaired.

"Hello?"

She started unpacking her groceries, placing the tea on an empty shelf. There was a lot of noise on the other end, the sounds of a loud, busy crowd or . . . drunks. Someone was calling her from a bar. Someone was drunk dialing her. Was it Frances? Finally coming around.

"Frances?"

"Hey, babe!"

Oh my God. There was only one man who called her babe, like she was his stewardess, waitress, escort, piece of ass.

"Daddy?"

"Yeah, I am just down the block from your new place."

The fear and dread were old reactions that came into being immediately out of habit. That's what being triggered was, she was learning, responding to the present from a place of the past. Sooner or later she was going to have to deal with this man, this *Wolf*. She'd known it in the back of her mind but had been pushing it to the side. The problems of *Daddy* always seemed better off delayed.

"How did you get my address?"

"You're listed."

"I'm listed?"

"Yeah, when I searched the white pages under your name, this address and phone number came up. You must have a landline."

Ohhhhhhhhh. The world spun.

So, Steven Brinkley had not *stalked* her. He had not followed her on the subway. He had not seen her walk in and out of a bar; he had not noticed her name on her mailbox. He had simply looked her up. And, of course, he couldn't phone her because the cables were down, and he really wanted to talk. He was trying to talk. He needed . . . he needed . . . some kind of . . . help.

"Come have a drink."

"Dad, you know I don't drink anymore." That felt *too* familiar, explaining the obvious to her dad about herself. Did he know that she was real? Of course not. How come Maggie didn't already understand this? Is every obvious thing on earth a big fat surprise?

"Well, then come sit with your dad while I have a drink. I'm lonely."

People, Places, and Things. "I don't want to, Dad."

"You're no fun. Maker's Mark Manhattan."

"What?"

"Just ordering my drink."

Maker's Mark Manhattan, that was Frances's drink.

"I gotta go."

"Maggie, you're no fun. No wonder you're still a virgin." Then he laughed.

"Bye, Dad, call me when you're sober."

She hung up.

The phone rang.

Frances?

"Hello?"

"I'm sober." He laughed.

"Guess what?" she said. "You're not." She hung up.

Why was Maggie so nice to her drunken father, who didn't have the balls to go to detox and rehab and AA for every second of the rest of his life? And why was she so mean to the flower guy? Projection!

The phone rang.

She answered it. "FUCK OFF."

"Maggie?"

"Wait, who is this?"

"It's Craig. Is that how you answer your phone?"

"Oh my God."

"Are you drunk?"

She could hear some kids in the background playing a video game.

"No, I thought you were my father."

"Great." Craig's voice returned from heightened, surprised disgust for Maggie to his normal level of general repulsion toward everything about her. "That explains it. Listen, I have been trying to get in touch with you all night. I left you four messages on your cell. Do you still have it?"

"Hold on." She found it at the bottom of her bag. "Yes, I have it."

"Is it on?"

She looked. "How do I tell?"

"Jesus Christ, you are unbelievable."

"I'm so sorry, Craig."

"Well, FIGURE IT OUT. Have you considered pressing the *on* button?" There was a little girl's voice in the background. "Honey, hold on. Not you, Maggie. My daughter's name is Honey."

"I can see how that could be confusing at times."

"Maggie, hold on. Have you seen the papers? Honey, hold on, I'm coming."

She stood still and waited for Craig to fulfill some paternal duty and continued unpacking her grocery bag. Warm yogurt, a bruised banana. One plastic knife. A newspaper. She laid it out flat on the kitchen floor. A typically blaring headline, a standard fuzzy photograph of some perpetrator or victim or both.

SCRIBE SUICIDES IN MURDER RAP

"What?"

"I didn't say anything. Okay, I'm back. Maggie, did you see the news?"

"I have it right here in front of me. Steven Brinkley committed suicide."

SCRIBE SUICIDES IN MURDER RAP:
"Her death was my fault," leaves note.

208

The newsprint felt like dust. Everyone was so fragile, humans. News is unreal when it happens to you, and entertainment when it happens to other people. Every single person in the world could self-destruct before their biology beats them to it. Some were trying to make that happen to others.

The last time she had felt this way was when she was in detox, on an IV, sick as a very sick dog, and two cops from Internal Affairs came to see her while she was still in bed.

"Maggie Terry?"

"Ugh." Every bone was aching. Her throat was so sore, it was on fire.

"When was the last time you spoke to Officer Figueroa?"

She thought they meant Eddie.

"When he graduated from the academy."

"This is not a joke."

She could barely lift her head from the pillow. "Does this look like a joke?"

"Your partner, Detective Julio Figueroa, was found shot dead at an apartment complex in the Bronx last week. The same one where his son Eddie allegedly shot a civilian. Do you know what he was doing there?"

Think fast, she told herself. She was sweating. Her feet were hurting. Her mind was hurting, and now her heart. Her poor, poor Julio. Her beloved, loved friend. She had let him down, and now he was dead. She was in here because she was such a fuckup she couldn't even make a stand with him, and now he was fucking dead.

"No, officer," she said. "I have no idea."

And she stuck to that story through three interviews, an official inquiry, the hearings. And even when the brass threatened her with charges for violating the regulation against working under the influence, she stuck to her insistence on ignorance. On innocence. And negotiated down to permanent removal and the loss of her badge.

Now, here she was again, this time on her kitchen floor, with a warm yogurt and another corpse on her hands. Another weeping, broken man asking her for help. Begging her to be there and she was nothing but a failure, a mess, a garbage-headed addict who couldn't reach out and help a friend. She remembered Brinkley's crying face through the elevator window, sobbing, *Please, please help me.* Why didn't she help? In Program they told her to ask for help. But when people ask her for help, they end up dead.

"Well," Craig said over the phone. "At least we know who did it."

She had to stop fucking up. She had to act. She had to *act!*

"I'm coming right over."

"Whooaa. Do *not* come over. It's nighttime. I'm at home with my children."

"Sorry, Craig, old habit. Police detectives are like trauma surgeons."

"Whatever."

She looked at her cactus. Yes, it belonged in the middle of the room until the day she got some furniture. She lay down on the floor. Someday maybe there would be a chair.

"Okay, Craig, so what do we do now?"

"We do nothing *now.*"

"I mean, tomorrow morning?"

He had a sharp intake of breath, as preparation for a gasp, wail, screech, or plain derisive laughing. "Duhhh, we close the case."

"Close it?"

"Yeah, read the article. Brinkley left a note saying that he was responsible for Jamie's death. End of investigation."

"He didn't mean it that way."

"*Really?*" he said with mocking sarcasm flowing out of his aura. "How *did* he mean it?"

"He didn't mean that he actually physically murdered her. He asked me to help him." She started peeling the banana.

"He asked you to help him kill her." Craig would have simultaneously believed and disbelieved everything she said, at this point, since he clearly felt he had a lunatic on his hands who was incompetent and yet capable of anything.

"No, he was asking me to help him not kill himself." As soon as she said it, Maggie knew it was true. Someone had asked her for help, thereby asking the wrong person.

"So, what did you do? Honey, lower that thing. No, sweetheart, we are still a democracy. What are you watching? You are too young to watch the news. Hold on."

"Nothing," Maggie said. "I did nothing."

CHAPTER TWENTY-TWO

11:30 PM

Crying, pacing, getting out of the house, running, going to an evening meeting, setting out chairs, raising hands, talking, listening to people, ignoring them, watching them, trying to watch a movie but not making it through, buying a television in a twenty-four-hour store with a salesman who helped her learn how to use it, carrying it home in the dark, feeling accomplished and considering that purchase to be a major step forward, and then sitting on the floor, watching that television set, feeling like nothing important had been accomplished, finally taking out those photos of Alina, remembering that time at the beach, taking her into the waves, holding her to her chest, anything, doing anything, being still, moving, breathing, holding her breath. None of the above would fix this or anything.

It was now too late at night to still be wide awake and stay out of trouble. She could not bear the sound of the TV, it was so noisy, it was so invasive. It was watching her. She paced the room, put on her shoes.

Don't do it.

Maggie stepped out of the elevator, walked up and down her block. If a man smoked crack or meth or whatever it was in that doorway then he bought it in that building, because no one bought crack or meth and then carried it around for an hour before smoking it. Maybe that dealer had some dope. She hovered in front of *that* building. Where was the action? Where was the action?

Maggie stared at every passerby. Where was that one going? Which one of them was high? Was anybody nodding? Was anyone smoking a joint? Who was holding? Who was holding? Who was holding?

A tired man with nowhere to go. Could it be him? He looked like an ex-student, now unemployed, some kind of fuckup. That was her type. Someone who had ruined everything too.

"Holding?" she said.

"Huh?"

"What you got?"

"You mean metaphorically?" He laughed.

No, not him.

She hurried away. He could call the cops. That's what everyone in this city did when they didn't understand what was going on. That's why so many people were being punished. No, *overpunished*. She did not have connections anymore. Too much time had passed. She did not know rich people, and rich people do their drugs in safety. Rich people order in their overpaid high-quality drugs from friendly dealers, who hand deliver. And they do them in the privacy of their expensive homes. And she didn't know them and didn't have their address. So, she had to buy from poor people, and they did their drugs in danger. Were there any streets in Chelsea that still had poor people?

She ended up by the projects on Tenth Avenue, some kind of Colonial Williamsburg of poverty in the middle of organic grass-fed steakhouses and glasses of Armagnac that cost a hundred dollars a shot. She didn't really know what that kind of wealth actually meant now, with its refined and muted excess. But *right* next door to Chelsea Market where one could buy Sarabeth sour-cherry preserves, and right next door to Equinox Fitness where movie stars went to do Zumba or whatever, right *there* was a housing project, which meant too many people in one apartment and unemployment and that meant dangerous drugs, not safe ones.

She saw him coming half a block away, and it was muscle memory. Of course this was the kid she was looking for. How could she think that other guy had the drugs? He didn't have them and this one did. What was wrong with her? How could she be so fucking stupid?

"Hey."

"Hey."

"What's happening?" She loved this. She loved being *down*. She loved the knowing and the recognition and the sharing of the secret, she loved that no one could stop her, and she loved . . . the ritual.

"I got C and D, Coke and Dope."

"You choose," she said, giddy.

She gave him the money, a young man. He seemed

bored and nice and distracted. He gave her a folded piece of paper. The pass-off was expert. Two experts. Their flesh never touched. He walked away. She walked away. And clutching the end of her failed sobriety, the end of the recovery that was never recovered, the end, the end, she started walking back to her apartment where hopefully they would find her dead the next morning, to snort whatever it was and let it all go.

End.

"Maggie?"

She kept walking.

"Maggie Terry?"

She turned. It was a lady cop in uniform.

"It's Tina Constanza."

"Heyyyyyy." She stopped, plastered a smile. "Hey, Tina."

"Everything okay?"

They were standing over a subway grate. The sidewalk was rattling, stale dirty heat swirling around her ankles. Maggie was inside an earthquake.

"You at the projects?" Tina knew.

"I was taking a shortcut back from the High Line."

"It's late."

"Yeah." She swayed with the vibrations of the train passing below. "You know the Artichoke Pizza place?"

"Oh, yeah."

"Well, sometimes you just . . . have to have it."

Tina smiled.

"Tina, you look great."

"Thanks, I put on some weight."

"Looks good."

Standing still was strange. It was like she was

flying, or more like hovering over the concrete. Over herself. It was cool outside. She'd just noticed that.

"Hey Maggie, sorry to hear about your troubles."

That was sweet. Someone knew she was in trouble and decided to rub it in. Tina was *sorry*.

"Thanks."

"How ya doing? Going to meetings?"

"Yeah."

"Me too. I've been sober, now, four and a half months."

Maggie tightened her grip on the C or D, but something in her shoulders relaxed.

"Eighteen months," she said. "And three, no four days."

"Congrats."

"Thanks."

"Maggie, it's kind of late for you to be walking around out here."

"What time is it?"

"After three. And Artichoke Pizza closed a long time ago."

"I'm on my way home, I had a bad date."

Tina smiled. She wasn't a smart girl. She wasn't a good cop. She was dirty and everyone on the force knew it. She took kickbacks and held on to cash and drug seizures and went on dates with women who should have been off limits.

"You're a nice girl, Maggie. And you had a bad time. Take it easy. Don't beat yourself up."

"Why not?"

"Because you can have better."

"Yeah?"

"Yeah."

What did Tina think she was doing? *Service?*

"Whatever you got in your fist, just open up your hand and let it go."

Maggie squeezed her hand tight.

"Just drop it."

The whole range of options ran through Maggie's mind. She could say *Don't tell me what to do.* She could run away. She could walk away. She could say *You're sick. You're the one who's sick. Nothing is going on here, nothing.* She could try to get Tina to break her sobriety, and stand in a shadow, snorting the white stuff together. It would be fun. They could be friends.

"Whaddya say?"

"All right," Maggie said.

Maggie opened her grip, let the dope fall beneath the iron grate.

"We gotta stick together," Tina said.

We, we dirty cops, we addicts, we white people. We of the special treatment and the double standards.

"Who's we?"

"Everyone who needs a fifth second chance."

And Maggie knew Tina was talking about herself. And that if they ever saw each other again, they would do coke and fuck.

She nodded. It was over now.

Silently, they waved each other on, and empty-handed, Maggie headed home down a quiet side street. Redeemed but destroyed.

DAY FOUR

SATURDAY, JULY 8, 2017

CHAPTER TWENTY-THREE

8:00 AM

It was pouring out and, as usual, Maggie had no preparation. She would buy an umbrella at Nick's. Running between raindrops, she felt a kind of comfort at having a regular first stop. Maybe it was working, this re-creation of a new set of habits, of places, of people, of things.

Darting in and out of awnings and construction overhangs, Maggie turned the corner, and then suddenly, something was very wrong. Had she gotten lost? It was only a block? Was she stoned? She racked her memory: Did she actually get high the night before? Why was she so confused? Where was she? Was this a dream?

And then that moment of shocked realization occurred, like when a person goes to feed the dog, but the dog is dead; when a man comes home from work, and the apartment door is open and the place has been ransacked; standing on the sidewalk holding groceries watching one's building burn to the ground; trying to remember where the car was parked to suddenly realize it has been totaled, or stolen. Maggie looked up at a dark, padlocked deli and read the hastily scrawled sign taped to the window.

Can't Pay the Rent. Thanks for Thirty Years of Business. —Nick

He was gone.

Are there ever real goodbyes?

Her witness had ended. She was aloft.

Finally understanding that she was really and truly alone now, Maggie let go of the last person who had known her *before*. The last caring, intimate, friendly face. She crossed the street to the cold-pressed juice place, and bought a cheddar scone, a soy latte, and a kale juice. And an umbrella. The check-out girl asked for twenty dollars. Maggie's old world was completely dissolved.

Saint Paul's was not as full as usual because of the rain. The weather sucked. It was daunting. Thunderstorms meant symbolic umbrellas that broke and twisted, rain ruined plans, outfits, haircuts, and brought stress, steamy sweat, discomfort, and mess. Some people make deals with themselves every day about whether or not they are going to go to meetings, and those people did not go when it rained. They could run out in the snow in their pajamas to score, but staying sober required good weather. Her plan for the afternoon was to buy a futon, and only use the sleeping bag as bedsheets.

New slogan: One Half Step, Every Other Time.

Omar was there. Martha was there in another sharp, corporate outfit. This one was canary yellow with a black silk blouse and a green scarf tied elaborately. Ramón's mustache was thickening. His eyes looked sad and his chin soft. Ronald, Alan, Karl, Charles, and a newcomer, Toshi, all appeared somewhat at peace. Even though Alan's share was whiny, it was calm. Monica had cut her hair into a wild shag that was supposed to telegraph *life* and *alive*, but she still seemed sad and tentative. Katarina, Sheila, Clifford, Chris, and Suzanne sat somewhere on the continuum from tired to contemplative, each with a puddle gathering underneath their dripping umbrellas. Marva was qualifying.

"Whenever someone really loves me," she said, "I flee. I blame them. I demonize them to justify destroying the relationship. Then, when my blame becomes unbearable and they respond, I use that to justify the blame. Retroactively. I forget which came first: their reaction, or what I did that created it. If I could really love you, I run. I hide in people who are as shut down as I am, or with whom the relationship can only ever be superficial. I fear equals. Not being seen is easier."

Maggie nodded. Then she realized what she was doing. *Identifying.*

Even though it was Saturday, Mike wanted them to all to stop by and celebrate. So Maggie's colleagues showed up in their weekend attire: Baseball cap for Craig, designer exercise pants for Enid. Sandy in an Indian print. At the office, there was a party underway. Fresh-squeezed peach juice. Trays of deviled eggs with caviar, blini with caviar, papaya salad, warm home-baked bread with freshly churned butter. Bowls of gray, red, and black caviar. Someone who wanted to show that they could afford to share caviar. Someone for whom caviar meant love.

"What's going on?"

"It's a party," Sandy said like it really was.

"Is it Mike's birthday?"

"No, no. He would never do something like this. Lucy Horne sent over a catered luxury breakfast for the whole office to thank us for cracking the case."

"But we didn't find anything."

Was that true? The real truth was that Maggie had passed up two chances to save Steven Brinkley. She could have had dinner with him, and she could have listened to his pain rather than making up a story about herself being the one in danger. She'd been around suicide before. She knew. She knew. She knew . . .

And the whole world stopped.

Her mother, of course.

Of course, her mother had killed herself. Of course, Maggie had devoted her career to other people's corpses. All that was long known.

But now, there was a . . . kind of enlightenment . . . an opening of understanding. Maggie's poor mother had ended her own life, rather than spend it with little Maggie Terry because . . .

Because she was drunk.

Her mother's life was unbearable, but so was Maggie's and she was still living it.

Why was it all making sense now, when it was . . . oh God . . . *so obvious*. Like a photograph coming to life.

Could she really have lived to the age of forty-two without ever actually realizing that her mother was drunk. She was drunk when she had committed suicide?

Her mother was drunk when she died. Maggie was only seven, and her mother had been drunk all the time. Her father was out fucking someone, and her mother was alone, sloshed, with the little girl, and Maggie wasn't cooperating—she was acting seven. Her mother was so overwhelmed, there was no one to call who hadn't already been called too many times, and she was angry about it. People weren't calling her back because they figured it was hopeless. No, actually they just didn't care. They were not thinking about words like *intervention* or about that little girl named Maggie. Her mother was so pissed off, so unable to bear it, so unable to integrate the information that her husband was a bastard and also a drunk, and instead her mother had become convinced that there was no way out.

In her drunkenness, she had become convinced that she would be stuck in that house with that kid for the rest of her life, always feeling as terrible as she felt that very second. So filled with drunken rage that it had all come to this. So filled with hatred that all her potential, her dreams, her trust . . . So drunk that she needed it to end right then and right now, she pulled open the kitchen drawer, the one closest to the liquor cabinet, and grabbed the knife they used for the Thanksgivings that had disintegrated into waves of cruelty, and she stabbed herself in the heart with that kitchen knife. That fury.

In a locked room, her final gesture of consideration toward her child. Locking the door. Leaving the mess for her drunken, satiated husband to come home to with his satisfied cock and satisfied balls and have to deal with his wife's intact face and torn bloody body below.

And yet, for some reason, Maggie had—all these years—thought of this intentional, delusional catastrophe as an *accident*. Some kind of accident. What is the definition of *accidental*? Something occurs that no one wants to occur; it is just an act of fate. It is not deliberate; it's a sidebar. A consequence unforeseen. Maggie's mommy didn't really expect her life to end. She was drunk. She couldn't think it through. It was an accident. She just didn't have anyone to talk to.

Did Maggie have someone to talk to?

She had those fucking 12 Step meetings. She had a sponsor.

It sucked, but these structures did exist. They were paltry and in so many ways impersonal. There was no romantic love there. There was no sex. There was no sleeping together, and holding hands. There was no using. There were no drinks. But there was still some place to go.

Maggie knew she would not have to kill herself. She was staying alive to protect Frances and Alina. She was helping them by staying alive. She would never have to do to them what her mother had done to her. Didn't they see that? She was refusing to shatter them while Frances was shattering her. It was a favor. That was what refusing to negotiate was like. It caused division and pain. It had consequences that never end and suicide was the ultimate refusal to solve a problem. And Maggie would never refuse to solve this one. She would live for the solution.

"Maggie? Maggie?"

She looked up into a sea of petals.

"And she sent these flowers." Sandy buried her face in the giant white lilies, just as Maggie had done with the roses she never took home. "Smell, Maggie." How did women learn to dive into flowers?

Maggie brushed her cheeks along the petals. She inhaled the scent of life, the natural world, its delicacy, its temporariness. How could people be so intractable when there are flowers? Why did she refuse to let Steven tell her his pain? Selfish. Asshole.

"And Lucy sent big presents. For each of us. Even me. Here, have some lobster quiche, it's amazing." A good receptionist is a caretaker. She handed Maggie a plate. "There is so much lobster."

Feast in hand, Maggie walked into Michael's office. She needed him to know what had really happened. That Brinkley's death was proof of *her* guilt, not his. It was her job now, to be accountable.

"Mike?"

Before her was the spectacle of Michael, Craig, and Enid eating caviar.

"And here is our girl!" Michael had a linen napkin on his lap, protecting his Armani suit. He had this air of *I'm doing it right* about him. A kind of salvation that can only come from exterior recognition.

"Maggie, wait until you see your gift basket." Craig had never shown her such enthusiasm before. Apparently, all was forgotten because of some gourmet products. And she realized that presents were *very, very* important to Craig. He had given her a phone, after all.

Enid resumed her conversation. "Can you believe, Mike, that he sent Ivanka to represent the United States of America at the G-20?"

Mike did not want to talk about it at the office, but he understood that Enid did. "It is all beyond anything resembling belief."

"They actually made Angela Merkel sit next to her. They should have sent that Barbie doll home to satanic Ken."

"I have a new name for her," Sandy piped up. "Ivanka Marie Antoinette Romanov."

"Well," Enid added. "I hope she meets the same ending."

"Listen, I think there is more to this case." Maggie was careful.

"Like what?" That was Mike, chewing on oysters but pretending to be open.

"No, there is *not*." Craig did not want her to fuck everything up, which was the only thing he had ever seen her do.

"I don't think Brinkley is the killer."

"Okay." Mike was listening.

"Whatever." Craig had already tuned her out.

"What is your evidence?" Enid was actually taking her seriously. That was the thing about Enid, she actually wanted to know what was true. That was her strength and her value. She looked at Maggie, waiting for her to present proof.

"I think he wanted to take care of Jamie and couldn't forgive himself that he had failed."

"That's not evidence." Enid returned to her peach juice.

"We have to keep the case open."

"Maggie." Enid had made up her mind. "I don't see any grounds."

"What is wrong with you?" Craig was finally exploding. All these examples of her ridiculous impulses, wrong guesses, and inept actions, and here they had *won* and she wanted to make it a loss. "You have been a liability from day one, and this is day four."

Liability.

"She has?" Enid turned to him like a parent to a nursery school teacher. "Has she been drinking?"

"I have not been drinking."

"I don't know," Craig said, finally putting down his fork. "She has inappropriate expectations outside the boundaries of office hours. She has bad judgment."

"That's how her partner got killed, you know. When they kicked her off the force. Showing up drunk at work. He *died*."

Maggie was teetering. Enid knew about that?

"All inquiries showed that I had nothing to do with Julio's death. It was not my fault."

"You were drunk on the job. And your partner died." Enid was on her now. "Do you think we're idiots?"

"Died?" Craig was trembling with rage. He finally realized how much danger he had actually been in.

Enid nodded. "A police officer. Drinking on the job, and who knows what else!"

This is how it works, Maggie knew. She did things that were very wrong, and there were consequences. But she did not do everything wrong. And every consequence was not caused by her and by her alone. These people were turning her into a specter, just as NYPD had done, just as her lover had done. Maybe if she had showed up sober that night in the Bronx, *maybe* she could have talked Julio out of his mission, but she doubted it. And she never would have been able to turn up sober. Most likely she would also have gotten shot, or even killed. Or perhaps her presence would have extended the fight and Julio may have murdered Martin Scott Bond, or maybe she would have become a murderer too. Or maybe they would have "succeeded" and intimidated the witness into illegally repressing evidence, and then they would have been real criminals, just like Eddie. Or maybe she, in her intoxicated, grand, distorted state, might have miraculously saved Julio's life, but that would have been an unlikely outcome since she was too out of it to have any realistic common sense. But no one could ever be sure if Julio Figueroa died because she was an addict, and in the process of being coercively hospitalized, and therefore did not keep her word. To her friend. Her beloved, sad, grief-stricken, desperate, confused friend who was worried about his son. His son who killed Nelson Ashford in cold blood, lived through a suspension, lost his father to murder, and then had the charges dropped by a racist in the DA's office and now was back on the beat. One thing did not equal the other.

"Maggie," Michael said softly, so quietly that he was barely making a sound. "Have you been drinking?"

"No."

"Okay, then. If Maggie says she has not been drinking, that is good enough for me."

She was not alone.

"You believe her?" Enid protested, but she also knew that this prosecution had been postponed.

Michael was going to help her.

"Of course, I believe her. Maggie told me the truth about my son that I refused to hear. If I had listened to her then, he would still be alive."

"You don't know that for a fact, Michael." That was Maggie.

"You're right again. I don't know that."

"Your partner got killed?" Craig still could not believe it. "No one tells me anything around here."

"That was not my fault."

"Maggie!" Michael shut down the bickering.

What was he going to do now? Fire her?

"Maggie," Michael said, calmly. "Make your case, and we will consider it. But you'd better have something there."

"Well." Maggie relaxed because this next moment would rely on her intelligence, not her judgment. "I have two questions."

"Okay." Michael reached for a yellow pad and pen, and pushed his oysters aside.

"My first question is: How did struggling actress Jamie Wagner, who lived in an awful apartment, afford to pay Florence, the energy therapist, two hundred dollars a session?"

Michael looked at the others. "Good question."

"Steven Brinkley wasn't paying it," Maggie reminded them. "He hated Florence and he also had an ethic about Jamie becoming autonomous so that they could have a more equal relationship. Her father is indigent."

"Okay, team." Michael enjoyed his ability to unite everyone. "Any answers?"

Craig brought his phone to his lips. "Speakerphone. Florence Black."

Everyone heard the ring. And then Florence's knowing voice.

"Hello?"

Craig held the phone out to Maggie.

The tide had turned.

Again.

CHAPTER TWENTY-FOUR
10:00 AM

"Hello, Florence?"

"Yes?"

"This is Maggie Terry."

She waited. Florence's voice crackled over the speakerphone.

"You and your husband are afraid of change."

"Exactly. Well, my husband and I have talked it over extensively. It wasn't easy, but we came to . . ."

Everyone in the office had their eyes on Maggie.

"He and I disagree about you. He's not convinced, but I believe you, Florence. I believe that you are the key to my healing."

"I am," Florence said calmly.

Craig scowled. He hated her.

"But I was wondering, is there any alternative to the two-hundred-dollar fee? Since I would be going on my own, and Craig doesn't want to contribute, do you have a sliding scale?"

"No, I make no exceptions. The more you pay, the more you invest in your therapy."

"Do you think my insurance would pay for it?"

"No, my methods are unorthodox and unique, and besides, insurance requires paperwork, and I just find that creates an obstacle, energetically. I become anxious about having filed the paperwork and it inhibits our exchange and communication."

"Well, what do you suggest?"

"I always say," Florence chirped, now that she was over the hump of being asked to give up money. "Try to find a relative to pay for your treatment. That's what I advise all my patients. There's nothing like needing money to bring a family together. People have to be nicer when they ask for money, and sometimes others feel better if they can help out."

"Okay, I will."

Maggie hung up the phone. It was so abrupt, the silence jarred her. But there it was.

Michael was grinning from ear to ear, he was delighted. He was literally bouncing in his wheelchair.

"Someone else was paying the bill! Maggie, you are brilliant! You are *so* brilliant. Find out who was paying this quack and we have our killer. Great job, Maggie." He was happy. He had been reaffirmed in his philosophy that, as a leader and a person, he had the responsibility to hear people out, even at the risk of discomfort.

"Okay." Craig was disgusted but knew the jig was up, and he had to get back in the game. "I'll locate Florence's banking records."

They all started clearing the paper plates, napkins, draining the last drops of peach juice.

"Wait." Enid stopped the action. "You said that was your *first* question. How did she pay the fee? But what is your second question?"

"Where," Maggie asked carefully, "is Jamie Wagner's *mother*?"

"Good question." Enid was sincere.

"Excellent question. We will get on that one as well." Michael pulled the napkin out of his collar signaling that the frivolity was over, and thankfully investigation, once again, was about to resume. "Everyone back to work. Maggie, I want to talk to you."

The others filed out, headed for their new assignments, and once they were gone, Michael took Maggie's hand and looked into her eyes. His were shaded by white eyebrows, she could see the hairs on the side of his brow.

"Maggie." He seemed very concerned. "Fix up your office. It is a mausoleum."

"Okay," she said.

"Do it now."

"Okay."

After lunch, Maggie came back with a large shopping bag.

"Did you get something nice for your office?" Sandy asked, either showing insight or having overheard the earlier conversation on the intercom.

"Yes, I did."

Sandy followed her down the hall. "What did you get?"

Maggie opened the bag and lifted out a potted cactus, identical to the one she had at home. It would be a comparison study. Which one would thrive, the public life or the domestic? Where would she be more respectful, more responsible, more caring? Finally, something to think about that wasn't connected to death.

"What a nice cactus."

Maggie placed it on her desk.

"Do you need a second chair?" Sandy suggested gently. "Maybe someone else will be here with you . . . someday."

Was that a come-on?

When the door closed behind her, Maggie approached her office window for the first time. There was a view, a wonderful view. The metropolis. The streets, the veins of the urban body. The transportation of feeling. There was so much possibility out there. Somewhere out there was another lonely woman, in a reasonable apartment, who had room for Maggie Terry. Someone smart and cute. Easy to be with. A wild side and a responsible side with a good work ethic, who she would respect, and therefore care for. Someone busy. Someone who could help her get Alina back.

She pulled out her phone and Omar's business card.

"Omar, it's Maggie. From Program. Hi, I would like to meet up for coffee. If you are still willing. After work would be great. My office is in Chelsea. I get home by seven. I'll call you then. Bye."

There was a knock at the door.

"Come in."

Sandy was back, staggering in with a massive gift basket. "Don't forget this, and Michael wants to see you."

Maggie walked into the conference room where Michael, Enid, and Craig were reviewing bank files.

"Maggie, look." Mike was happy. "Look what Craig found, you were right. Several two-hundred-dollar checks deposited in Florence's account by one Louisa Wagner."

"Her mother," Enid conceded. She looked Maggie in the eye. "You were right." Enid was sorry.

"Her mother." Maggie had lived so long in the land of the missing mothers that she hadn't considered the obvious. "Jamie has a mother somewhere who loves her, who cares for her, who supports her, who wants her to get better and be happy. There *was* one person in Jamie Wagner's life who she let love her. She had hope. She should have lived."

"That's a nice fairy tale." Enid's contrary approach was now familiar, not threatening and even somewhat endearing. "I have four children and I can attest that mothers can only save the day in fairy tales. In real life, someone needs to rescue mothers from their children and save us all from our mothers."

"No mother would ever voluntarily abandon her child." Why was Maggie hearing herself be so shrill? She was getting all emotional just as she had crawled back into the group's good graces. *Sabotage.* Sabotage.

"Craig," Enid generously avoided the confrontation, "I am continually disturbed by how much information you can get on everyone, and how quickly."

"That's why I get paid the big bucks."

It was a save. Enid was saving her from ruining everything again. Enid was being a friend.

"Hear me out, Enid." Craig looked over with some compassion. She was old and didn't have a clue; Maggie saw that gloss of youthful information in his eyes. "The government knows everything about you now. Edward Snowden and Chelsea Manning risked all they had to let us know how much the government really knows, and how little protection we actually have. Corporations understand *everything* about you: what kind of porn you watch, what kind of hair-growth products you use, they know every fear and curiosity that you have ever googled. The police know your retina shape. So, Enid, you need to adjust your thinking. It can't be that the normal status quo is unimaginable for you, or you will never be effective again. If all your foibles and flaws are legible, so are everyone else's. Why do you need that illusion called *privacy*? Ask yourself what you are hiding. Let it go."

"But I don't want anyone to know."

"Consider it an opportunity," he said. He had a theory about this and now he had found the occasion to explain it, to show them how valuable he is. How much they needed him if they were going to understand and be functional in their own world. "Before, everyone was lying about what they were doing. We were all pretending we were exceptional but we were all doing terrible things and hiding them. Now, the ship is transparent. Everyone's mistakes are legible. So, we can't pretend anymore that we are clean."

"Thank you, Craig," Maggie said, feeling seen and moved.

"Not you." Craig laughed. "You aren't like everybody else."

CHAPTER TWENTY-FIVE

6:00 PM

Maggie staggered out of the building onto Eighth Avenue, barely able to keep her outstretched arms firmly gripped around her enormous gift basket. Craig toddled out after her, trying to catch up but weighted down by his own lucre.

"Hey, Maggie, hold up."

She stopped, hoping he wanted to be friends. Perhaps he knew that he had been mean and was ready to take it down a few notches. After all, she was sure he had googled the police commission report, so he knew they *officially* ruled that she had nothing to do with Julio's death. Even though that was a lie. She wanted to be Craig's friend. She needed a straight-guy buddy in the world, who was smart and responsible. And since Mike had paired them together, they were going to be collaborating and there was a lot of room for camaraderie there. Craig had issues, but who didn't? He was just uptight and might learn a thing or two from her as well. Julio had been the rock in her insane life, until insanity reached his. They provided each other with routine, and routine bonds people. It is the basis of community and a feeling of trust, which is why people with business to work out have to have experiences together. Share them. See that there is something good.

"Hey, hold up." He was panting, overweight, sluggish.

"Hey."

"I found some info as you were on your way out."

"You mean that I was cleared by the police commission in Julio's death."

"No, I found that out at 10:33 this morning."

"Okay, what then?"

"Maggie, I called you on your cell."

She was sincerely sorry. It was time to grow up. "I'm sorry, Craig. I haven't had a moment to figure out how to retrieve messages. But it *is* on."

"It's time for you to learn."

"You're right." She nodded. And he *was* right.

"I know you are interested in the Ashford case," he said. "And I think I understand why. Just letting you know that the family filed charges in civil court today."

"What can that do?"

"Well the cop who killed their father can't go to jail. But the NYPD can pay out large fees. It's better than nothing."

"Thanks for the update. Anything else?"

"Yeah, it's about Jamie's mother."

"Louisa Wagner."

"That's the thing." He tried to shift his gift basket to

balance on one hip while reaching for his phone. "Her name isn't Louisa Wagner. It's Carrie Moyer. She's a piano teacher in Albuquerque, New Mexico." The reward slipped to the ground. "Whew." He sweated. "I'm taking a cab."

She watched him ride away as she heaved her burden of gifts into a wider, tighter grip and started toward her apartment, pausing on every other corner to take a break and breathe.

Eighth Avenue was looking very unloved. All the places she and Frances had passed on a daily basis were dead, and their corpses were long gone or still rotting in the gutter. The old corner liquor store in a Civil War–era building was gone; Rawhide, the gay cowboy bar was long gone. The gay porn and video store was for rent. The long line of overpriced restaurants that had always lined the block were hanging on, with the last remaining old gay men consuming margarita happy hours and egg-white omelets. Next to them she saw the young couples—straight and gay, they were equally obnoxious—move into these new high-rise condominiums, housing projects for the wealthy. They were nondescript, derivative, and elite, with lobbies that seemed from a distance like an upgraded Marriott. It was all so ugly and so bland.

And suddenly Maggie felt that she was getting better. She was developing taste and standards, likes and dislikes. She was starting to care. And maybe she would have to move soon. To a real neighborhood that she could relate to. Maybe nearer to Frances. They had to work it out. Then she could live down the street, and Alina could come over after school and do her homework. It all made sense. It was reasonable. And therefore, it could be.

She paused on another street corner, balancing her gift basket on a wire trash can while catching her breath. She would never give up on Alina like, her own mother did, like Jamie's mother did, abandoning her, leaving her in the clutches of that crazy father. Jamie Wagner, Jamie Wagner. Her mother was not her savior. Think, think. Maggie had to focus. Be Jamie. Pay attention. Think like Jamie. Breathe. Get inside of Jamie's mind.

I have been manipulated by the sick mind of the person I love the most in the world, my daddy.

I finally meet someone who wants to help me get better, to face it, to become an equal party in love.

But as soon as I open my heart to him, I feel he is going to annihilate me.

The way my daddy did.

I'm in a rage about my life.

I can't sleep.

I am dissociated.

I am blaming the person who can help me heal.

My life is a fog of pain.

I go to a therapist because she doesn't tell me anything that I can't handle. And I can't handle very much.

Therefore, I never get better.

Pain. Pain.

I blame it all on my lover who is truly there for me. I can't bear his care.

I shut my father out but I still can't sleep.

My mother has fed me to the wolf.

Every night I come home from the show, have some

Chinese takeout on my fold-out couch, in my window-less apartment, and listen to the mentally ill man downstairs yell at his mother.

I can't have real friends because they will see that something is wrong.

That I am like my father. Sick.

So, I tell Steven that he's "the sick one." That I am going to have him arrested, because no one ever had my father arrested. I want Steven in jail because he is the dangerous one. He makes me feel and I can't stand to feel that deeply about someone else, because then I will care about all the pain I am causing him and I don't have room to care. He makes me feel something that I can't handle, something real. I'm in so much pain that I can't sleep. What do I do? What do I do? What do I do?

And then Maggie realized.

I have a drink.

She stepped out of the cab, gift basket first, and looked around. East Eighty-Second Street off of Second Avenue was also generic, but in a slightly different way. The decay here was one of compliance. Heterosexual families and single white women. It was the same bad food, the same overpriced restaurants, but a different kind of despair, one without community. There were still some old people in rent-controlled apartments and very few good places to buy fresh vegetables. It was rotting in the very particular way that Manhattan had started to rot.

Maggie stood in front of Jamie's building, set her giant gift basket on the concrete to rest.

Okay, it's night.

Jamie had gotten off from work and bicycled home from the theater district, locked her bike to the front gate. She ate her dinner. There were sleepless hours ahead of her, and she needed a drink. She needed some way to calm down and to be with people without them knowing her secret. That she was suffering.

Maggie turned her back to Jamie's building and looked up and down the block. To her right was a brightly lit pizza place. Directly across was an old tenant, a tailor. He wouldn't be there much longer. And then, diagonally down the way to the right, she saw it. A bar. It was so close. Jamie didn't even have to cross the street to stumble home and flop on her bed. Maggie got closer. The Red Den. She carried the basket, and opened the front door to a wall of laughing, glasses clinking. It was packed. Three deep at the bar.

No, Maggie reasoned. This was not the place. It was too social. Jamie would want something quiet, anonymous, and manageable. She would seek out a bar where she could watch TV without being bothered. Where she could be alone in public with her suffering. She would go out to be alone.

Maggie stepped onto the curb again, looked back up and down the block.

There it was.

Right next to the tailor's. So beaten down and out of sorts that the window wasn't even illuminated. It was hidden, wounded and endangered. Like Jamie.

Maggie walked over, confidently. There was no life, no activity. Only when her face was up to the door did she notice its name, The Keg, painted on the glass. When she pulled open the heavy door, she was hit with a blast of stale air. She walked into silence. The place was a crypt, a hole for the spiritually dead. It smelled of mold. The lights were low. The TV was on, tuned to a bad station. It was so sad, she could hardly breathe. Every dream and plan that had been hatched in this room had come to nothing. This was a den to stay in for all four seasons. The perfect place to live a lie, the lie that encases and controls life. This is the lie that makes a person repeat and repeat the painful decision that someone else who loves her was hurting her, that she didn't have a right to a real life. Night after night Jamie came here so that she would never have to change, so that she could hold tight to the lie that she was not really loved.

CHAPTER TWENTY-SIX

7:00 PM

"So, she was midtwenties, attractive but depressed, emotionally transparent, a young—"

"You don't have to go any further," the bartender interrupted. "There was only one young lady who ever came in here on her own. I know exactly who you're talking about."

He was an old guy who had probably been a kid in this neighborhood when it was still Yorkville and filled with Irish and Hungarians and Germans, both Nazi and Jewish. He grew up surrounded by wurst shops and marzipan and paprika. Probably his father owned the bar, or his uncle, and by now they had all drowned in beer as this man soon would. These days he was exhausted, no matter how late he slept, too tired to fix this place up or advertise or even really clean. The only nod to present day was Sam Adams on tap. Otherwise Bud, Miller, Miller Lite. His top shelf was Johnny

Walker Red, Gordon's, and a bottle of Jack Daniels. He was a shadow and night was falling.

"She came in all the time, after work. Three or four nights a week. Talked a lot. What a nutcase, a heartbreaker—you know, charming, sweet, really. Pretty. But scratch the surface and she was out of her mind, you know what pretty girls get away with."

Maggie examined herself in the cloudy mirror behind the register. "A damaged beauty."

"You said it." He leaned on the bar for dear life. "Vodka and cranberry. Lonely girl. Very lonely. Really needed someone to talk to. She'd come in, have a few, and get very angry."

"At you?"

"No, I know how to handle them. She was pissed off because some guy was bothering her."

"When did you see her last?"

"She came in and got sloshed pretty fast, ordered another vodka and cranberry—which is a kid's drink. For people who want Kool-Aid in their alcohol."

"Like cosmos," Maggie added.

"Exactly." The guy warmed up to Maggie because she was a drunk, after all, and bartenders need drunks like firemen need fires.

"What did she say?"

"She was telling me about this guy, how she finally told him off big time, let him know she was going to call the police."

"Did you hand her the bar phone?"

"Not at all." The guy smiled at himself. All the things he'd seen, all the tricks he knew, how none of them mattered anymore. "I told her to call the cops when she was sober. It would be more effective. And she smiled and said, 'I'm an actress, don't forget. I can play sober.' And she started acting out a pretend phone call."

"What do you mean?"

"You know." He mimicked talking on an invisible phone. "She held her hands to her face like she was holding a receiver, and in this kittenish voice, 'Officer, sir. Please put my daddy in jail.'" Then the bartender changed his demeanor. He became dead serious. "That was the first time that I realized her problems were with her *father*."

"Yeah."

"See, I thought all this time she was talking about her boyfriend. So I said, *Your father?* And she got really upset. It was a slip. She didn't want anyone to know. She said she was going to be a big TV star someday and she couldn't have anyone knowing that her father was a predator."

"What did you say?"

"I told her the truth. That I couldn't care less. I only watch sports anyway." He gestured over to the silent game on the ancient TV. "But she wouldn't let it go. She got dramatic, hysterical; she got flushed and looked like the poor kid was going to fall apart. She was overreacting like mad, which was annoying, but she was so sincere about it, it was distressing. It made you want to comfort her any way you could."

"Could you?"

"Nah, it was too far gone. She made me promise, so I promised. I swore, raised my right hand and swore to God. And here I am telling you. But she's dead, so rest her soul."

"Did she believe you?"

"Not really. Even after I promised, she wouldn't let it go. She said, 'If anyone finds out, she will strangle me. She said so.'"

Wait a minute.

"*She?*"

"Yeah."

"Jamie told you that a woman threatened to strangle her and then she got strangled and you never called the police?"

"Look, I figured out that sooner or later they would get their asses over here." He shrugged. "And you did."

"I'm not the police."

"So, I'm not in trouble."

Maggie felt bereft. "She knew she would be strangled."

"Things happen. Hey, you look upset." His eyes were big red saucers of compassion. This man did not like to see others hurting. "Here, have a drink. On the house." He poured a Sam Adams from the tap. The good stuff.

Maggie looked at the glass of beer. She remembered Sam Adams. It was smooth and toasty. She could almost chew it but it was soft, a blanket around her cares, and sweet and cold. Like something someone's mother was supposed to bring them in bed when they couldn't sleep. But this balm was for adults who could never sleep because the person who brought them their milk was crazy.

"No thanks," she said. "I guess not."

"Oh, have it your way." He took the beer for himself.

She picked up her gift basket and started out the door, looking for another cab, wishing she had those things on her phone that made getting them so easy. She leaned back into the taxi's soft seats and looked out as they traversed the city. Down Second Avenue, and then across Twenty-Third Street.

In Manhattan every twenty blocks is a mile, and this stretch, from Eighty-Second to Twenty-Third had nothing to offer. Nondescript restaurants. Where was she going to move to? Did it have to be Brooklyn? It was so expensive. Maybe Queens. As soon as she and Frances started talking, Brooklyn would be the place, but if she moved there too quickly, the police might start calling. They had never tracked her down. Maybe Frances was bluffing or canceled the call. Maggie hoped so. Maybe they told Frances to go fuck herself and grow up and learn how to negotiate. That there were real crimes going on out there, like children being kept away from their mothers. That would be sweet. When should she move to Brooklyn? That was the question. Before or after Frances and she started to talk. It was inevitable, a healing. Sooner or later she would soften. Maybe someone had to die or something that put it all in perspective, but Frances had to grow up at some point. She couldn't do the wrong thing forever. Could she?

The big problem was Maritza, and there was no way around that. Every time someone made an intractable stand on immoral grounds, they did it because they had some cheerleader whispering in their ear to "go get that bitch," telling them that what was wrong was actually right. Without that person, Frances would be bothered by the truth. She would come around. But as long as Maritza was invested in Maggie being the one and only problem, Frances would be rigidly fixed on doing the detrimental thing.

By the time she got home, she was in a frenzy of despair. Maggie paced back and forth, going crazy in her tiny room. The cactus, the fucking gift basket she had carried all over the city. There was hardly any space to pace. It was late. She was suffering. It was endless. It would go on forever, the injustice of the whole situation. When would it turn around?

Her cell phone rang.

Now what?

What the fuck did Craig want now?

"Hello?"

"Maggie?"

"Yes?"

"Maggie, it's Omar."

"Omar?"

"I waited for your call for two hours. This time you did promise."

"Oh my God, Omar. I am so sorry."

He's making me accountable.

"I debated calling you," he said. "But I know that we are both committed to being clear and reliable."

"Thank you so much, Omar. I really appreciate that."

She sat down on floor where the futon would go.

"I am so, so sorry."

She started unwrapping the gift basket.

"You were so right to phone me," she said. "Something came up at work and I wasn't being conscious and aware about my promises."

She unwrapped the cellophane, took out a papaya.

"I want to be a person who keeps my promises."

She pulled out some tiny bananas.

"Omar, I would love to keep talking for a bit now. Would that be okay?"

"Sure, that's okay." He was nice.

"Thank you."

She pulled out two mini pots of jam. One was sour cherry and the other was peach.

"So, Omar. What did you do today?"

"Well my partner Jacques and I went to Central Park this morning, just to do it. Now that we don't drink anymore we have all this free time. Mornings *and* evenings. We want to fill it with experiences, like the gardens in the park in the early dawn."

She took out a fancy imported mustard.

"That sounds great. Then what did you do?"

"Well, Jacques is a nurse, so he went to the clinic. I used to be a teacher before I ruined it with my addictions, so it's been hard. But now I have a steady job at Macy's, which is good."

"He stood by you."

"I'm so lucky. People need a break."

"What kind of teacher were you, Omar?"

"I taught Arabic language and literature at NYU. I was a grad student. I didn't complete my work and stopped going to class. I was depressed and getting high instead of facing and dealing with my problems. My goal is for them to forgive me and allow me back into the degree program. What about you?"

She took out a bottle of pure, organic maple syrup and one of Kirschwasser.

"I'm a private detective and—"

She gripped the bottle.

"Hello? Maggie?"

She stared.

"Maggie? Are you there? Are you still there?"

"I gotta go."

"Maggie? Maggie?"

DAY FIVE

SUNDAY, JULY 9, 2017

CHAPTER TWENTY-SEVEN
5:OO PM

"The Music Box is the Broadway theater that every playwright yearns for. Small, sophisticated, welcoming, prestigious, and intimate," said the young man clutching his Playbill outside the stage door.

"Are you a playwright?" Maggie asked.

"Oh, yes. But I haven't had a production since 2007. It's a terrible business. I write a play every year, but nothing. I keep writing them, though."

"Why do you keep writing if you can't get them produced?"

"Because," he fluttered, somewhat ashamed and somewhat proud, "one *might* get produced. I just can't risk missing that chance."

"I understand."

Then she had another question.

"How do you deal with Trump? With the confusion and the cruelty and the lies and the disintegration of a nation that had been trying for so long to get better? How do you put that into a play?"

"Beats me," he said. "I like musicals."

An older woman clutching a Playbill butted in. "I heard today that his son Don Jr. got caught lying about a meeting with some Russians. That could be a musical."

"I don't know," the young man answered. "It doesn't really sing."

The crowd had been waiting for over twenty minutes, but they didn't seem to mind. Many of them were stage-door veterans, and some were there every single night. If the public understood how many Broadway tickets were sold to obsessed fans with repetition compulsion, they might have a different view of the Great White Way.

Finally, the door swung open and out came the supporting cast, including the former understudy, Kat Klarke, whose career had been launched by Jamie Wagner's murder. Like her predecessor, she knew her place and quietly walked through the ignoring crowds, invisible. Her chance to be adored, projected onto, paid, and distorted by attention lay before her. What would it be? Sod or celebrity?

Maggie knew that when looking at the big picture of a bad situation it always made sense to evaluate who had the most to gain from any crime. In this case, there was only one person's life that would be materially enhanced by Jamie Wagner's death. And that was her understudy. Instead of rotting backstage, had Jamie lived, Kat Klarke was now seen every night by everyone who came to see Lucy Horne. And that is what actors want to be, isn't it? Seen?

But the second important consideration when trying to solve a crime is to understand that people also do things that don't benefit them. In that immediate moment, perhaps, there might be a catharsis, but the sad fact was that most serious crime is committed by people who don't really think ahead.

The crowd parted to facilitate Kat's disappearance and went back to waiting for the object of their devotion. Finally, the stage door opened again, but this time the throng stood on their toes, they were so elevated by the in-person experiences that theater provided. It was the special evidence that they were alive, in front of each other, at the same time, together. This understanding was enough to have brought so many of them to New York in the first place—whether for the evening, the week, or the rest of their lives.

Then Lucy Horne swept out. The crowd sighed. She smiled, fully aware of the cameras but never pandering to them. She signed five programs, flirted and withheld. She basked, she was loved, she gave and connected and looked into the eyes of people who had never been noticed before. She reached out and touched and she performed *generosity, compassion, empathy.*

"Louisa," the plainclothes officer called out.

She looked up.

We have her, thought Maggie.

It was inadvertent, wasn't it. The response. If she had been at all suspecting, the word *Louisa* would have had no meaning, but it had very much meaning because it represented everything about herself that she hated and wanted hidden. This was the name her mother had called her, and her horrible father, on the boat when they had come over as children. Little pitiful refugees, both of them born in the rubble of occupied Berlin, in a displaced person's camp. Who knows what her father did during the war? It could have been anything. He was a sadist. And *Louisa* was what her very sick brother called her, until she'd beat it out of him— *Lucy, Lucy, Lucy.*

And why in the hell did she ever give that girl a chance? It was Stefan, threatening and begging, following her, sending letters to every location. *Help Jamie; Help Jamie.* The girl was talented, and in a moment of fatigue and weakness, she said *yes*, she could audition. And then the director liked her, and she was fine, and only once the show opened did Lucy come to understand what a time bomb she had on her hands. That this girl was sick. And she couldn't keep anything to herself, and she spilled that Stefan, that they *talked* about inappropriate things, to a degree that was . . . scandalous. It was illegal! It was something that Disney would never understand. No one would understand. And then that stupid girl fell in love with of all things . . . a writer. And writers write what they see—Lucy learned that the hard way—especially when treated unfairly. And any fool could tell he was good for her, that writer, he loved her. And Jamie's life had a chance, but she couldn't bear the authenticity, she started acting out against him, and Lucy knew where this was going, that he would end up writing about her sick brother and the sick girl, and Jamie swore she hadn't told him they were related, the same sick family. But then she started threatening that she would tell him . . . what did she call it . . . *the truth.* That she *had to,* if they were ever going to build a life, the fool, that she would take down the entire existence of the great Lucy Horne, her whole past and her whole future, and she was unstable this girl, and if Jamie ever let her boyfriend know that her sick, criminal father, and Lucy were brother and sister the writer would tell. He would tell *the truth.* She knew Jamie would make him crazy, and he would try to understand, that even if it took years, he would grapple with it and grapple with it, and finally, one day, just to have some peace from all her accusations and craziness and blame, one day the writer would tell.

CHAPTER TWENTY-EIGHT

Maggie took the R train to Seventy-Seventh Street in Bay Ridge, Brooklyn, and walked down Third Avenue. It felt like New York, if New York was a small town. An old-fashioned soda fountain that wasn't vintage, but just actually still there. Some bars. An ancient dance academy that taught flamenco. Turkish food, Palestinian food, lots of dates and basmati rice. Down the side streets, Arab and Latino families were out playing cards in the heat, each one with a front yard and some had old porches. How long would it be able to stay this way?

When she got to the right address, she saw him immediately, right there. He was hanging out, smoking a cigarette, drinking a Bud Lite, alone in the night. He'd put on some weight, and gotten older, of course he had. They had both been through so much.

He was staring up, where the stars should have been, and she could hear the birds that he could hear.

"Eddie?"

"Yeah, who's that?"

She walked up closer, so he could catch her features in the streetlight.

"It's Maggie. Maggie Terry."

Eddie Figueroa's face widened and paled with surprise. He stood up, arms outstretched, and staggered toward her. He might have had a knife in his back, that's how stung he looked. He came closer, and closer. He stared at her. She expected him to fall over and crush her.

"Eddie, I'm so sorry about—"

Eddie hugged her so hard that he became her. Their breasts were pressed, flattened against each other's chests.

"Maggie, they dropped all the charges. I'm back on the beat."

He was so happy. It was a victory. He was dulled.

"What a relief for you, Eddie," she said.

"Thank you." He was shaking her hand now. Shaking it really hard. "Thanks, Maggie. How cool of you to come by."

"Eddie," she said. "Your father was the best friend I ever had."

And then, she couldn't do it. She couldn't say, He died because I am a drug addict and an alcoholic. I lied to the police commission. I am a liar. I let him down.

She couldn't say it because she would be telling it to the wrong person. Because Eddie was a killer, and so was she. They were both on the wrong side, the lying side. And in some horrible way, they both paid a terrible price, but they both still got away with it. They both had the chance to live.

"You want to come in and have a beer?"

"No, thanks. I was just in the neighborhood, so I thought I'd stop by."

"Oh, yeah, what are you doing in Bay Ridge?"

"Having dinner with some friends. At that Palestinian place."

"Okay, then." He was so happy. He was the winner. "I'll let you go. I'll tell my mother you were here."

"Okay, goodnight, Eddie."

"Take care."

And he disappeared into the shadows.

Then she got back on the R train, took it to Union Square, and changed for the 4 train. There was good air conditioning in the cars, but not on the platforms. It was a Sunday night in the summer and people were pretty low key.

Maggie got out and followed the instructions she had written on a piece of paper bag, and walked some underlit, empty streets until she reached her goal. It was a hot, rickety street, awkward metal doors in different stages of unbalance. Uneven steps. Unsynchronized storefronts, held together by gates and shaky metal sheets. This was where it all happened. This is where it all took place.

Some old black men were playing cards on a folding table on the sidewalk, near a pushcart selling *piragua* in three sweet grayish flavors. It was very quiet. An ugly dog lay sprawled on the concrete.

There was some kind of West Indian music coming from the apartment, and people were talking inside.

She knocked on the door.

A woman in the middle of a conversation came close to the door and looked through the peephole. There was the sound of locks turning, and the door slid open the length of a chain. The young woman's eyes, her brow, and the bridge of her nose peeked through.

"Yes?"

"Mrs. Ashford?"

"Yes."

"My name is Maggie Terry."

"Yes."

"I used to be a police officer."

"The police?" The woman clucked with disdain and then fear.

Maggie looked in the eyes of this stranger. It was time to make amends.

"I am here to see if I can help you get some justice. I want to do what I can to help make things right."

And, finally, it was all on her.

THE END

ACKNOWLEDGMENTS

Thank you to the Corporation of Yaddo and the Mac-Dowell Colony. Special thanks to Tayari Jones and Jeffrey Van Dyke, and gratitude to Rakesh Satyal for your invaluable help. An impactful subway conversation with Nan Boyd was a great influence on this piece. Thank you to my editor Lauren Rosemary Hook, Linda Villarosa, and everyone at the Feminist Press.

The Feminist Press is a nonprofit educational organization founded to amplify feminist voices. FP publishes classic and new writing from around the world, creates cutting-edge programs, and elevates silenced and marginalized voices in order to support personal transformation and social justice for all people.

See our complete list of books at
feministpress.org